ANDROMEDA SNOW
SUPERHERO

ANDROMEDA SNOW
SUPERHERO

JAMIE LACKEY

ISBN: 979-8-9850216-0-8

I woke up in a small, unfamiliar room, feeling indescribably weird.

I woke up in a small, unfamiliar room, feeling indescribably weird. Some kind of succulent was wilting on the bedside table next to a dusty old picture of me and my sister. Various intimidating machines loomed over the bed, beeping and whirring. The walls were an industrial beige, the lights buzzing florescent. But it was the smell that let me know for sure that I was in a hospital—bulk cleaning products just barely overpowering a whole battery of unpleasant human scents.

I stood up.

A nurse came in with a cup of coffee. She closed the door and leaned against it with a sigh. Then she saw me. She dropped her coffee.

I started to say hello.

The nurse screamed and ran.

I tried to follow her, and that's when I noticed that my arm was too thin, that I couldn't feel my feet against the floor, or the doorknob when I tried to turn it. And then I freaked out and threw the bed out the window with my brain.

• ○ •

When I woke up again, I was in a tiny room lit with a single lightbulb dangling on a long wire. I glanced down at my body and saw that I was still wearing just the hospital gown, and that I was strapped to a chair. But I couldn't feel anything. I did have a sense of my body, in a way, sort of a kinetic awareness, but I couldn't feel the chair pressing against my legs or the cold metal under my fingers. I touched my nose with my tongue. I could feel that.

It wasn't much, but it was something.

A woman with a clipboard and a stack of folders walked in. She was like a living stereotype, every pretty librarian ever all crammed into one spectacled brunette. "I'm Dr. Vivian Sherman. I'm in charge of this facility."

"Hi," I said, trying to keep my voice calm. They probably wouldn't untie me if I was hysterical. "I'm Andromeda Snow. But you probably know that."

"Yes." She flipped through a folder. "What is the last thing you remember?"

I blinked at her. "The hospital. The bed. The window."

She nodded, then walked behind me. "Well, that's good. And before that?"

The memory came to me, burned into my brain. I reminded myself that I couldn't be hysterical. "I was driving. It was cold, had just started snowing. A deer darted into the road. I braked, but there was an oncoming car. They swerved. I think they missed the deer, but they hit me. My car went off the road, down over the hillside. It rolled a few times.

"I was trapped in the car. I couldn't move. It was cold. I thought I was going to die. Then nothing. I must have passed out." I remembered hanging upside down, tangled in my seat belt, my head pounding and blood dripping into my ear.

I hoped the deer was okay.

"Yes," Dr. Sherman said, still behind me. "You did pass out. The other driver called 911, but you were unconscious when the paramedics arrived. And you've been in a coma for just over two years."

Two years? "That can't be right."

"Your spinal cord was severed. You're completely paralyzed from your C5 vertebrae down."

"No," I said, shaking my head. "I can move." To prove it, I wiggled my fingers. I knew they were moving, even without looking, even though I couldn't feel them drumming against the arm of the chair.

"Yes, well. From what we can tell, that's telekinesis. It seems like you've automatically replaced your normal sense of proprioception with your power."

"Telekinesis isn't real," I said.

"It is now. It's been an... eventful couple of years."

"This is insane," I said. I took a deep breath, then let it out. Calm. I was calm. I was a mountain pond. Maybe I was dreaming.

"Where are we?" I asked. It was a distraction—I didn't want to think about being paralyzed or missing two years of my life. I really didn't want to panic, but it was getting difficult. I focused on my breathing.

"We're in a secure government facility. We needed to be able to contain you, since we weren't sure if you were cracked."

"Cracked?"

8

"Superpowers can be hard to deal with. About one out of every five people who gain powers go crazy. About half of those are violent."

"And what happens to those people?"

A door opened, and Jeff fricking Appleton—international superstar, former tennis pro and Academy Award nominee, named sexiest man alive at least three times—walked in the room. He was wearing navy blue tights and a navy and yellow shirt that could have been painted on.

I couldn't help noticing that his eyes were just as blue in person as they were on all of the magazine covers.

"If people are cracked, we deal with them as humanely as possible," he said.

"As humanely as possible," I repeated. "What does that even mean?"

"Usually, lifetime detention," Dr. Sherman said.

And that was the moment that the reality of it all hit me.

I was telekinetic.

I was paralyzed.

It had been two years.

The superstar in the tights was a superhero.

And I was going to be a superhero, too, damn it.

• ○ •

Joining a super team meant signing a lot of paperwork. Dr. Sherman escorted me out of the holding cell, and we were in a small, windowless conference room. "So, Jeff Appleton is a superhero now?" I asked.

"Yes. He's the team leader. He's in charge of training and decisions on the ground. I keep the whole facility running and deal with the larger-picture issues."

She looked at me over the rim of her glasses. "Try not to be too star-struck. You'll be working fairly closely with him. Do you think you can handle it?"

I nodded. He was incredibly attractive, but I was engaged. Or at least, I had been. I wasn't wearing my ring, but maybe it has fallen off my weirdly skinny fingers.

Dr. Sherman slid a tablet toward me. "Here are some ideas for possible costumes."

Half of them seemed to involve miniskirts. "You have to be kidding," I said.

Dr. Sherman shrugged. "I know, some of them are pretty silly. We're given a set of standard designs."

The color schemes were all yellow and navy blue—our super team's colors—and mostly spandex.

"I want Kevlar," I said. "Or chain mail. I can't feel anything, I want some fricking armor."

"I suppose that is a valid request," she said. "Let's table your uniform for now. Why don't you tell me why you want to be a superhero?"

"Well, I guess I just want to help people."

Dr. Sherman nodded and jotted something down in her notebook. "Any idea of how you want to do that?"

"By fighting evil?"

She laughed. "Okay. We'll make that your mission statement. How do you feel about seeing your loved ones? They know that you're here, and two of them are lurking in the lobby."

"The shady government building where you bring potential superpowered people to kill or indefinitely detain on the down low has a lobby?"

"There is no 'down low.' Everyone knows the risks involved with superpowered individuals. The basement is a secure facility. Above ground is the team's official headquarters."

"Right," I said. Asking about the building was stalling. Again. Dr. Sherman probably knew that. I got the feeling she knew lots of things. "Do you have powers?"

"Just one."

"What is it?"

"I'm a touch telepath."

"So, you can touch someone and read their thoughts?"

"Exactly."

"So, why didn't you touch me?"

She arched an eyebrow at me. "I did."

I'd had no idea. No sense of her fingers on my skin, no sense of her touching my thoughts. It felt like a violation. "I really want that Kevlar," I said. I needed another distraction. "What did you do, before?"

"I managed a chemistry lab. When my powers manifested, they decided I was an ideal candidate for this job." She gave me a wry smile. "It's mostly paperwork."

I'd been a waitress. "Did anyone think that I'd wake up?"

Dr. Sherman shook her head. "The doctors weren't optimistic."

I glanced down at my right hand, to where my engagement ring should have been. There wasn't even a tan line. Had Conner waited? Or given up? There was really only one way to find out. "I would like to see my family. But could I get some real clothes first?"

●○●

Dr. Sherman gave me a navy t-shirt and sweatpants. Both were a little big. I could see the sweats sagging on my hips, but I couldn't feel them. I tried not to think about it.

Jeff Appleton, still in his spandex, accompanied us to the lobby. "You can call me Jeff," he said, giving me his million-dollar smile. He had a dimple in his right cheek that I'd never noticed. "It's good to have you on the team."

"Um, yeah. Thanks. Jeff. No secret identity, huh?"

He shrugged. "Nope. Our identities are a matter of public record. And coming up with a good superhero name that hasn't already been taken in the comics is really difficult. It's not really worth it."

"I think this might be the first time that I've been glad that my parents named me Andromeda."

He laughed. Jeff Appleton laughed at my crappy joke. Dr. Sherman gave me a wry look, and I did my best not to be 'too starstruck.' "Are you still acting? Or just being a superhero full time?"

"Just the superhero thing. I like helping people."

His smile really shouldn't be legal.

The elevator doors hissed open. The lobby was a huge open space, all marble and gold with tasteful navy accents.

And there was Conner, standing with his hands in his pockets, next to my sister, Cassandra. My two favorite people. And they looked so right, standing together without me between them.

11

I didn't even need to see my ring on Cassie's finger. Superpowers hadn't cracked me, but this might.

"Dr. Sherman," I said, forcing the words past the lump in my throat, "why didn't you tell me that my fiancé and my sister were together?"

She blinked at me. "Did you want to visit them separately?"

Jeff put a hand on the back of my neck. I could actually feel a little over half of his hand, warm and dry against my skin. It was the first time I'd felt someone else's touch since I woke up. It helped.

"Take a deep breath," he said. "It's okay. It's reasonable for you to be upset. You're not going crazy."

The awareness that I felt of my body expanded, and I could sense the whole building around me, each stone sitting on the next. I could pull them all apart, if I wanted to.

I took a deep breath.

Jeff squeezed my neck gently. "You don't have to do this if you're not up for it," he said.

Then Cassie spotted me. Her face broke into a grin, and she ran toward us. Conner followed, but slowly, and his face looked just like it had after that time he ate a whole plate of expired convenience store burritos.

Jeff kept his hand on my neck until Cassie's hug pulled me away. Her cheek was wet against mine, and her hair still smelled like the same cheap shampoo. "I can't believe it," she said. "You're awake. And moving!"

"I'm telekinetic," I said. I felt like I was carved out of wood. A woman turned into a statue.

"That's... amazing," she said, and I tried to ignore the flash of fear beneath her joy. "They told us that you'd never wake up. I'm so happy that they were wrong."

Conner hung back, looking uncomfortable. "Look, Andi," he said. "I'm really glad you're awake. But there's something that we need to tell you."

I reminded myself that they'd had no reason to believe that I'd ever wake up. That without my power, I'd be trapped in a bed for the rest of my life. "What is it?" I asked, even though I knew.

Cassie couldn't meet my eyes. "Conner and I—we're—"

"We're engaged," Conner said.

They were engaged, and I wasn't. Just like that. Conner and I had been together for six years before he even proposed. And we'd been engaged for three. If I threw in the years of the coma, that was over a decade of my life. Part of me wanted to insist that they break up, that they honor my prior claim. Part of me never wanted to see either of them again.

They were both staring at me, fear and pain clear on their faces. "Congratulations," I said. My voice sounded far away. I pushed Cassie away, aware of how easy it was to move her, aware of how her whole body stiffened in terror. I lifted myself up into the air.

And despite everything, the fact that I could fly filled me with a ridiculous joy. "I'm going to be a superhero."

● ○ ●

Dr. Sherman took Cassie and Conner away to talk about logistics or something, and Jeff walked me back to the elevator. "Are you okay?" Jeff asked. He looked legitimately concerned.

I managed to nod. "How did you know?"

"Know what?" he asked.

"About them. About me."

He shrugged. "I'm good at reading people."

Something he had over Dr. Sherman, apparently. I took yet another deep breath. Blaming her wasn't fair. "Thank you, Jeff." Using his name felt a little more normal.

"Is there anything else I can do to help?"

I shook my head. "I'd just like to be alone for a while. It's all been lot to process."

He nodded. "I get it. Let me know if you want to talk, though."

I blinked back sudden tears. "Why are you being so nice to me?"

"We're going to be a team," he said. "Why wouldn't I be nice to you?"

"You're a movie star. Aren't you supposed to be aloof?"

"Well, I did start out as an athlete."

I laughed, and the lump in my chest loosened just a bit. "Arrogant, then."

"Oh, I am that. Ask anyone. As soon as you're over your trauma, it'll be all about me."

"I suppose I should take my time, then."

He smiled at me. "Take all the time you need."

● ○ ●

After she was done talking to my family, Dr. Sherman walked me to my assigned room. "When I asked about your possessions, I was told that your things were donated to charity."

"Oh," I said. I told myself that it was for the best—that I was starting over with a fresh slate.

"Also, your care over the past years accrued a considerable cost. We'll handle the expense, but I'm not able to provide any additional advances on your salary."

"Okay," I said. The paperwork had mentioned something about pay, but I hadn't read it as closely as I probably should have.

"Are you feeling any pain or discomfort?"

I shook my head. I didn't feel anything at all.

She sighed. "I wish I had some better news for you, Andromeda."

"Yeah, me too."

She opened a door and waved me inside. "This is your room, it's yours to decorate however you wish. Once you have anything to decorate with, that is."

"Thanks," I managed.

"I wish I could stay and help you settle in, but I have a mountain of paperwork to get through. But if you do need anything, my office is down on the third floor."

"Okay," I said.

She left, and I spent about ten minutes staring at the blank gray walls and trying not to cry. Then I spent about an hour curled up on the bed, sobbing.

Cassie and Conner were getting married. All of my possessions were gone. I couldn't feel the bed beneath me. I didn't know what day it was. I wasn't even sure what year it was. I felt unmoored and lost.

Then my stomach rumbled, and I realized that I could still feel hungry. And then I realized that I had to pee. I went to the bathroom, grateful for the unconscious control my power apparently gave me

14

over my body. I didn't really know what things would have been like without it, but I imagined it would not be very pleasant.

I splashed some water on my face, noticed that I looked like utter crap, then decided that didn't matter. I took a couple of steps, then lifted myself off the ground and floated down to the cafeteria. The floating was pretty awesome, and it helped. I sat by myself with a couple pieces of pizza.

Jeff sat down next to me. He'd finally changed out of the spandex, which was a bit of a relief. Though he was still incredibly hot in his jeans and plain black t-shirt.

I was testing to see if it was easier to just move the pizza, or to move my body and pick it up with my hands.

It was much easier to do it with my hands. My own body was the easiest thing to move—as long as I didn't think too hard, my body just worked.

I was 100% sure that Jeff knew that I'd been crying. I was trying not to think about it. After a few minutes of silence, he offered me one of his French fries.

"This is going to sound terrible, but please don't take it the wrong way," I said, after I accepted the fry. "But don't you have any friends?"

He laughed. "What is the right way to take that?"

I shrugged. "As a compliment, I suppose. I would have expected you to be surrounded by people."

"You missed a lot," he said, his voice soft. "There have been enough incidents with people who cracked that most people aren't comfortable with superheroes. That's why our identities can't be secret. It's why we all live here. And the rest of our team members are pretty young. Like, teenagers young. They're great kids. But they're kids."

"Dr. Sherman isn't a kid."

"That's... true, I suppose. But she's here to monitor us. To make sure we don't crack under the pressure of it all and turn into monsters. She's not exactly friend material."

"So, becoming a superhero drove your old friends away, and none of the rest of your super friends are old enough to buy liquor."

"Exactly."

"So, you're lonely and desperate."

15

"Desperate probably isn't fair, but I'll give you lonely."

"So, what is there to do? Is there a place for us to practice?" Jeff nodded. "There is."

I finished my pizza and stood up. "Let's go."

• ○ •

"Okay, try to catch this with your power," Jeff said, tossing a baseball at me.

I caught it.

Jeff frowned. "With your power, not your hands."

"Moving my hands is using my power," I said, rolling the ball from one hand to the other. It was weird to watch my body move without any physical sense of it. I couldn't feel the rough stitches or smooth leather. I couldn't tell if the surface was warm or cool.

I wasn't going to be able to feel hot showers or cool sheets or fluffy kittens.

I blinked hard and took a deep breath. Then I held the ball out and lifted it off of my hand, so that it hung in the air. "It really is like magic."

"Good. Now, catch this one."

• ○ •

Our teammates were literal teenagers, and Jeff introduced me to all of them over breakfast the next morning.

Seventeen-year-old twins Teresa and Tabitha Wu, one could control fire and the other water. They had light brown skin, brown eyes, and long black hair held out of their faces with matching headbands. They looked up at me, exchanged a look that I absolutely could not read, and gave me matching welcoming smiles.

Landen Jones, who was nineteen, a little on the short side, and solidly built, with shoulder-length sandy hair. He looked like he'd be a good hugger, and he could talk to animals. He had a pet chipmunk perched on his shoulder and the effect was disarmingly adorable.

16

Jackson Duke, our youngest member at fourteen, who was tall and black and thin, with close-cropped hair and a shy grin, who could fly and turn himself invisible.

And me, with my telekinesis, and Jeff, who was super-strong and nigh-invulnerable.

"How are the teams organized?" I asked, sipping my coffee and looking around at our rag-tag group. I missed the feel of warm ceramic between my palms. "I mean, our powers aren't exactly a set."

Landen shrugged, and his pet chipmunk ran from one shoulder to the other. "It's geographic. Each major city has a team, and anyone who gets powers and doesn't crack is automatically assigned to the closest city's team. We can request reassignment if we want."

I frowned. "What if someone doesn't want to be on a team? What if they want to just keep living their normal lives?"

"That's not an option," Jeff said.

I decided to just let that line of questioning go. It's not like I didn't want to be here, after all. "Why are you all so young? Did all the older members request reassignment?"

The kids exchanged a look, then all stared at their respective cereal bowls. Jeff pushed his hands through his perfect hair and sighed. "No one requested reassignment."

The silence stretched. The kids ate cereal. "What happened?" I asked.

"We had a fight against a super villain," Jeff said. "We defeated him, but we lost people."

"He could make poison gas," Jackson said. "It didn't hurt Jeff, and they had the rest of us stay back. He wiped out an entire city block before Jeff stopped him."

"I wish I could have had everyone stay back," Jeff said. "But I couldn't stop him alone."

"That sounds horrible," I said.

One of the twins, Teresa, I think, shrugged. "Lots of horrible things have happened. But we're still here, and we have to just do whatever we can."

They ate in silence for a few minutes. I drank coffee and ignored the toast that Jeff slid toward me.

17

"So, Jeff says that you're paralyzed, that you can't feel anything from your neck down," the other twin, hopefully Tabitha, said. "Is that true?"

I nodded.

"That's rough," both twins said in unison.

"And your sister is marrying your ex-fiancé?" Jackson asked.

Another nod.

"Also rough," Landen chimed in. "You should take Jeff as your date to their wedding."

Jeff choked on his toast.

"Ooh, that's a good idea," Teresa said.

"You think so?" I asked.

"Of course," Tabitha agreed. "He's essentially the ideal date in this situation."

Jeff buried his face in his hands. "I did not put them up to this."

"I don't even know if they're going to invite me."

They all gaped at me. "You think they might not even invite you?" Teresa asked.

I shrugged. "I suppose they will. It would be pretty rude if they didn't. But I might not go. It would be super awkward."

"There's a superhero pun there, and I just want you all to know that I'm resisting it," Landen said.

"You have to go," Tabitha insisted. "You have to show them that you're the bigger person, and that their betrayal doesn't bother you."

"And that you've already moved on to a superior new beau," Teresa said, waving at Jeff like he was the prize on a gameshow.

I frowned. "Doesn't that seem a little petty?"

"You'd have to take one of us, no matter what," Jackson said, his voice soft. "We're not permitted to travel on our own." He smiled at me. "I'd be happy to be your date, if you'd prefer."

Jeff gave them all a flat look. "Are you all done hazing Andromeda?"

The kids all rolled their eyes.

I opened my mouth to tell them to call me Andi, then stopped. I'd never liked my full name, but maybe it was time to embrace it. After all, it was a better superhero name. And another line between my old life and my new one. I wasn't Andi, anymore. She'd died in that car in the snow. I was Andromeda.

●○●

"So, not to pry, but do you not have other clothes?" Jeff asked, the second day I came down to breakfast in the same ill-fitting sweats.

I blushed and stared down at the sweatshirt. "No. My family got rid of all of my things."

Jeff pinched the bridge of his nose. "That is unacceptable." He finished his toast in three huge bites. "Come on, you're not going to eat anything anyway. I'll get you a coffee."

"Where are we going?"

"Shopping."

"Jeff, I don't have any money."

"I have plenty."

"I can't let you buy me a new wardrobe."

"I'm lonely and desperate, remember? Think of it as a bribe."

We walked out of the building into the early morning sunlight. The air smelled like fall, and that unmoored feeling swooped back into my belly. The last time I'd been outside, it had been the middle of winter. How different would my life be if I'd just left work a little earlier? Would I still have powers? Would I have died fighting some supervillain? Or would I be living a normal life, married to Conner?

A small crowd of angry protestors crowded together on the sidewalk and shook signs that said things like *Supers are Terrible* and *Put Down the Powered*. A few signs were just pictures of ruined cities. They were all different cities.

A small blonde woman threw an egg at us.

I caught it with my power, and the crowd gasped.

"Monsters!" the blonde woman screamed. "How dare you show your faces in public!"

I opened my mouth to say something very scathing about her face and probably also her mother, but Jeff grabbed my elbow and pulled me into a car.

"What was all that about?" I asked.

"They call themselves 'The Protectors of the Mundane.' People don't like it when other people are different," Jeff said. Then he sighed. "Also, supervillains have killed a lot of people. And lots of them started out as heroes."

19

"Do you know anyone who's cracked?"

"Yes." Jeff said. But his tone didn't encourage more questions, so I dropped it.

I let him buy me coffee and a new wardrobe. I didn't look at the price tags, but the places he dragged me to were considerably fancier than the Goodwill, which was where most of my old wardrobe had come from.

Not that anything I owned would fit my coma-wasted frame. My hip bones stuck out like angry knives, and my wrists didn't look like they should be able to support my hands.

The whole thing was surreal. It all felt like that scene from of *Pretty Woman*. Well-dressed women kept bringing me things to try on and cooing over how lovely I looked.

But trying on clothes is weird when you can't feel anything. I had no idea if something pinched or rubbed. If a pair of pants was comfortable or uncomfortable.

At least everything looked like it fit.

And no one else had thrown anything. A couple people had even asked Jeff for his autograph.

"So, do you think it's about time for your dramatic haircut?" Jeff asked.

I laughed. I'd always kept my hair long. "Let's do it."

He took me into a salon where they gave us each a glass of wine and a tiny box of gourmet chocolates. The back wall was covered with this beautiful waterfall fountain thing, and the air smelled like flowers.

"I want to look like a badass," I said.

My stylist, a middle-aged woman with seven earrings in one ear and bright purple, spikey hair, just grinned. "I can do that."

She was just turning me around to examine her handiwork when Jeff's phone started playing the Superman theme.

I had an instant to look at myself. The lower half of one side of my head was shaved, and my hair swept down to chin length on the other side. I was just deciding that I liked it when Jeff pulled me out of the chair.

"There's a fire," he said. "We have to go."

●○●

The kids didn't look like kids in their costumes. It made me wish that I'd taken the time to get mine right. Jeff, apparently, wore his under his normal clothes. They looked like a team, standing together in their navy and yellow spandex.

"We're pretty good at fires," Jeff said. "This is really just a good chance for you to see us in action."

So I stood next to the firetruck and watched.

An old apartment building blazed in front of me. It was four stories tall, built of crumbling red brick with fire escapes that looked unsafe for small pets.

I could feel the heat on my face, and the acrid stench of smoke filled the air. The fire was loud, and I could hardly hear the team and the firefighters shouting over it. Teresa stood a few feet ahead of me, her arms stretched out to the dancing flames. Jackson hovered over the building, shouting instructions to Tabitha, who was pulling water from the firetruck and sending it where Jackson pointed. A small flock of birds darted in and out of the building, apparently reporting any trapped people to Landen, who sent Jeff in after them.

It did seem like a good system.

I had no idea where I'd fit in. But I wanted to. I wanted to be a part of this team.

I extended my senses, trying to sense the apartment building the way I'd sensed our headquarters on my first day.

It was harder when I wasn't angry. There was no way I was going to be able to feel the whole building, so I concentrated on Jeff. He was running in and out, careless about his own safety, using his body to shield anyone he was carrying.

He picked someone up. Someone heavy. His feet started to break through the weakened floorboards. So, I caught him. He had a couple of other bad moments on his last few trips—the building wasn't exactly structurally sound.

It also wasn't on fire anymore. Teresa and Tabitha were leaning on each other, and Jackson settled to the ground beside them. "Nice job," he said.

"That was really amazing," I added. "All three of you."

21

Jackson blushed. "Fire duty's been our thing for a while."

"I can see why."

Jeff and Landen joined us. "We got everyone out," Landen said. "No major injuries. Some minor smoke inhalation, a few cuts and bruises, a couple minor burns."

"Andromeda, was that you spotting me in there?" Jeff asked. "I didn't know you could do that."

Now it was my turn to blush. "Yeah, it was me. You're welcome."

"What did she do?" Jackson asked.

"Caught me a few times when the floor gave way beneath me."

Landen scowled. "We've told you to be more careful about that, Jeff. You're invulnerable, but the people you're carrying aren't."

"That's not what is important right now," Teresa said. "Andromeda. Your hair. It's awesome."

"Come on, guys. Time for the traditional post-fire pizza," Jeff said.

The rest of the team cheered, and they looked like kids again.

•○•

I stared at my new haircut, moving it strand by strand with my mind. Between that and the coma-induced weight loss, I hardly recognized myself.

I wasn't a fan of the gaunt look, but at least the haircut did make me look like a badass.

Someone knocked on the door. I assumed it was Jeff, and opened it with my mind.

Tabitha stood in the doorway, a shy smile tugging at the corners of her lips. "Hey," she said, stepping inside and pulling the door closed behind her.

"Good morning, Tabitha. What's up?"

She flashed me a full smile at that. "Are you guessing, or can you already tell us apart?"

"I can tell."

"Part of your power?"

I hadn't really considered it, but it was true. Tabitha felt different than Teresa, somehow. "I guess. I still have a lot to figure out."

She nodded. "About that—with the whole being paralyzed, I thought that maybe you should have someone checking you for cuts and bruises and stuff. At least till you're sure enough of your power to check yourself."

It was a good idea, and probably something a doctor should have suggested. Did we have a regular physician in addition to Dr. Sherman? What was she a doctor of, anyway? I wondered suddenly if superhero work came with medical insurance. I really should have done a better job reading the paperwork over.

"Thank you. That's a really good idea."

"Our grandma is diabetic, and she can't feel her feet. She almost lost a toe because of a blister. I don't want that to happen to you."

"Should I just strip down now?"

Tabitha nodded. "I figured we could get into a routine before bed, but I might as well check now, just in case."

I've never been particularly modest, but having a very fit teenager study every inch of my post-coma, mid-thirties body was pretty much mortifying. Still, I stood with my arms held out to the side and my feet shoulder width apart as Tabitha walked slowly around me.

"Hmm," she said from behind me.

"What?" I asked. I was hoping she wasn't going to point out any cellulite and ask what it was.

"Can I touch you?"

"Yeah. Thank you for asking, though."

She knelt down behind me. It was weird, knowing that she was touching me somewhere that I couldn't see.

"There's a red spot here, on your hip."

I craned around to see it, and extended my power to try to sense the spot. I couldn't feel or see anything out of the ordinary.

"It looks like maybe something you were wearing was rubbing there, just a bit. It's probably nothing, but I want to cover it and keep an eye on it." She chewed on her left thumbnail. "I'll go grab a bandage for you, hopefully that'll help." She stood up. "Stay put, I'll be right back."

While she was gone, I looked around the room. Jeff had had yesterday's purchases sent up, so shopping bags dominated one corner. But other than that, it was just basic, dorm-style furniture. I wondered if the others had decorated their rooms.

23

The bedroom that I'd shared with Conner had been cluttered with books and dirty laundry, the walls covered with pictures of the two of us and posters from shows we'd been to together. Surely he hadn't thrown all of that out? Had he really tossed all of my books, all of my cds and dvds?

I wasn't dead. But he'd apparently acted like I was.

I could feel the whole building around me again, and took a deep breath. I started hanging my new clothes in the wardrobe in the corner, working on fine control, draping each garment carefully over the hanger before carefully hooking it into place.

Tabitha got back before I was halfway done. I positioned myself so I could watch her work in the mirror. She cleaned the spot with peroxide, slathered it in ointment, and carefully bandaged it.

"You're good at that," I said.

"Thanks. I was thinking about going into nursing, before."

"Is that off the table now?"

She shrugged. "I guess not. It's complicated, though. I can't just take normal classes, knowing I could get called out at any moment. I can't really get a job doing it, since superhero work will always come first."

"Well, why not be the team medic? It seems like we could use one. No one else thought of checking me for injuries. You did."

She smiled. "Maybe. I guess I could look into some online classes. You coming down for breakfast? We usually all eat together before we train."

"I'll swing by for some coffee once I'm dressed."

"Cool, I'll see you down there. And I'll be back tonight, before bed."

"Sounds like a plan."

● ○ ●

I finished hanging up my new wardrobe, picked out something to wear, and headed downstairs. Tabitha was finishing up a bowl of cereal, Teresa was demolishing a pop tart, Landen was feeding bits of toast to his squirrel, and Jackson was sitting down with a waffle and a pile of bacon. Jeff was making himself an omelet on a single burner hot plate.

24

I got myself some coffee.

"You really should eat something," Jeff said.

I rolled my eyes.

"Do you want an omelet? I'd be happy to make you one. Or you can have this one. It's got ham and cheese and green peppers in."

"He's never going to stop," Landen said, his voice pitched low. "Just give up. Get some toast or something."

I rolled my eyes again, but made some toast.

Landen winked at me, and his squirrel scampered over.

"Don't think I don't see what you two are doing," Jeff said, giving both me and Landen flat looks. "Don't whine to me when your energy flags at 10."

"Sure, Mom," Landen said. "Whatever you say."

"I certainly hope you mind your mother better than you do me," Jeff grumbled over his eggs.

"Hurry up," I said. "Isn't it time to train?"

Jeff finished his omelet in four huge, deliberate bites. Then we all trooped to the training room.

It was my first time training with everyone else, and I kept getting distracted from my own assigned tasks, watching Landen talk to a shark or Teresa create a fiery tornado that swirled around her. Lifting things and setting them back down wasn't nearly as interesting.

Still, I did it. The plan was for me to lift larger and larger things, till we finally got to something that I couldn't pick up. By the time I was lifting cars, I'd stopped paying attention to anything but the task in front of me.

I could lift a fully loaded semi-truck. I don't know where Jeff found a tank, but I couldn't quite lift it. I could still push it, though.

When I was done, I felt drawn out and exhausted. My body felt sluggish when I moved it—I felt like I was pushing it through a wall of pudding.

I lowered myself into a chair and looked up to find all of the kids staring.

"Damn," Jackson said. "That was pretty impressive."

I managed a smile. "I think I might have overdone it, though."

Jeff handed me a bottle of water, and I managed to drink it in shaky gulps.

"You hungry?" he asked.

25

I nodded. I could really go for some pudding. Or a steak. Or anything, really.

"How about you, Landen?" Jeff asked.

"I'm okay."

"That's because he had his squirrels bring him a sandwich," Teresa said.

"I could go for a sandwich," I said.

"Well, go ahead up to the cafeteria. The rest of us will be up after we wrap up."

I stood, but my hold over my body wavered, and I wobbled on my feet.

In a heartbeat, Jeff was there. He picked me up like I weighed nothing. "Jesus, you really did push it, didn't you?"

I couldn't move. I fought to keep panic out of my voice. I was getting really good at not panicking. "I want a sandwich," I said. "And some pudding."

"Okay, okay. Let's get you to the cafeteria." He turned to the rest of the team. "I'm trusting you guys to finish your exercises."

Teresa rolled her eyes. "Sure thing, Mom."

Once we were out of the room, I turned my face into Jeff's chest. "I really, really overdid it," I said, my voice muffled.

"That's probably my fault," Jeff said. "I should have saved the tank for next time."

"Jeff, this is serious."

My face shifted, and I could only assume that he was squeezing me. I wished I could feel it. I took a deep breath. "I can't move."

"Not at all?"

I focused, and managed to flex one finger. Dark spots danced in my vision. "I think I just need to rest. Food will probably help."

Once we got to the cafeteria, Jeff sat me carefully on the floor, leaning against the wall, then got me dish of pudding. He fed it to me, spoonful by careful spoonful.

I blinked back tears. The whole situation was insane. "I hate this."

"I'm sorry! I figured chocolate was safe. Do you want vanilla? Or butterscotch?"

I laughed, and a couple of tears did escape and roll down my cheeks. "I didn't mean the pudding. The pudding is great. I mean not being able to move. You having to feed me."

"I don't mind," Jeff said.

"It would be really easy for me to rely on you way too much."

"I wouldn't mind that, either."

"Parents! We finished our homework!" Teresa, Tabitha, Landen, and Jackson burst into the cafeteria.

"Why is Andromeda on the floor?" Tabitha asked.

"I didn't want her to fall off of a chair," Jeff said.

"Oh, did she overreach?" Jackson asked. "I did that right after my emergence. I tried to stay invisible for a full day, and then I appeared in front of my sister when I was in the middle of stealing her—her Halloween candy. When I tried to fly away I fell out of her window. Luckily her room was on the ground floor."

"How long did it take for it to come back?" I asked.

"A good night's sleep is usually enough to recharge." Tabitha knelt down next to me and tucked her folded sweatshirt between my head and the wall. "Do you want me to move your arms? They look a bit awkward."

"Yeah, thanks."

She crossed them across my stomach. She turned to Jeff. "Do you want me to feed her?"

"I've got it."

The kids pulled chairs into a rough semicircle around us and ate from plates balanced on their laps. Teresa looked from me to Jeff, arched an eyebrow, and smirked knowingly. Landen had a squirrel fetch me a sandwich, and Jeff cut it into pieces and fed it to me. Jackson told us a few more stories about his early exploits, and Tabitha kept going and fetching me pillows that I couldn't feel.

It felt like a family.

•○•

Dr. Sherman knocked on my door the next morning. "You've got mail." She held out a cream colored envelope. I recognized my sister's handwriting.

I held out my hand. I could move again this morning, though my body still felt heavy.

Dr. Sherman put the envelope in my hand, and I watched our fingers touch. I wondered if she'd done it on purpose. If she'd reached into my mind.

27

"How are you settling in?" she asked. "Is everyone making you feel welcome?"

I remembered Jeff, carefully tucking me into my bed, then Tabitha, coming in after to check me for any injuries. "Yeah, the team is great."

Dr. Sherman beamed at me. "That's great."

"So, should I be in contact with a doctor or something?" I asked. "I don't really understand my injury or what it means."

Dr. Sherman shifted uncomfortably. "The doctors who were in charge of you before have refused to continue to treat you. They don't work on supers. I've been trying to find a replacement, but it's taking time."

"I see," I said. I didn't really. But I also didn't really want to deal with it.

"It's not like you're trapped in a chair or in pain, though, right?" Dr. Sherman said with an encouraging smile.

"Yeah," I agreed. "Things could be worse."

"Do you want me to try to get you in touch with a support group? I imagine that dealing with your disability alone is difficult."

"I'm not alone," I said. "The team has been a great support." It wasn't like I was really disabled. Not being able to feel anything was terrible, and not understanding exactly how my body worked and what it could still do or not do was frustrating, but I had it so much better than so many other people. "I'll be fine," I said.

"If you say so," she said. "Let me know if you change your mind."

I turned my attention to the envelope in my hands. The fine cream paper was edged with gold. I imagined its texture, smooth and satiny under my fingers. There was really only one thing it could be.

Dr. Sherman hovered in the doorway, still smiling.

"Thanks again for bringing this," I said.

"It looks like a wedding invitation," she said.

"You think?" I couldn't keep the sarcasm out of my voice.

"Would you like me to stick around while you open it? Do you need emotional support? That is what I'm here for."

I tried to appreciate the thought, but I really just wanted her to leave. "Thanks, but that's okay."

"Okay. But if you change your mind, or just need to talk, my door is always open."

I nodded, and closed the door. I went and brushed my teeth and washed my face and got dressed.

Then I opened the envelope slowly, carefully separating the glue from the paper with my mind. I pulled the invitation out.

It was the same heavy cream paper, with gold lettering.

For just a second, it hurt less than I anticipated. Then it didn't. The gold letters blurred. I might have screamed. I dropped to my knees and wept.

My first date with Conner had been in college. We went to a movie and ate cheap pizza and talked about whatever we'd been learning in philosophy class. We'd moved in together after graduation. I thought that I'd be growing old with him.

My door came off of its hinges. Jeff stood in the broken doorframe, clutching it by the handle.

I looked up at him and tried to say his name. I managed a broken sob.

He dropped the door and came to me. He ran his fingers through my still-unfamiliar short hair and let me cry into his chest.

I don't know how long we stayed like that, but eventually my tears slowed. My eyes stung, and my whole head ached. "I've always hated crying," I said. "And now that my head is pretty much all I can feel, it's even worse." My voice sounded small and stuffy, but at least I could form words again.

He kept carding his fingers through my hair. "Do you want to tell me about it?"

"I got my wedding invitation."

"Ah."

"I know it's dumb, but—"

"It's not dumb. You have every right to be upset. Anyone would be."

His shirt was wet from my tears and almost certainly snot. I sat up and looked at him. He reached forward and wiped a stray tear off of my cheek. My face felt like an absolute wreck, and he was still here. Still looking at me like I mattered. "Would you be willing to come? As my date?" I hated how small and hesitant I sounded.

Jeff's smile was like the fricking sunrise. "I'd love that."

29

I smiled back at him, a tiny bit amazed that my face could still do that. "My sister had a poster of you on her wall when we were in high school."

"But not you?"

I laughed. "I wasn't into tennis."

"Was she?" he asked.

I laughed and shook my head, because she really hadn't been. She's just been into his abs.

"Seriously, I'd be honored to accompany you. Like the kids said, you'd have to take one of us, anyway."

"I'm sure Jackson would look dashing in a suit."

"Andromeda." He wiped another tear off of my cheek.

"I don't understand you," I said. "Why are you so interested in me?"

"My love life has been splashed across the world since I was a teenager. It's never been easy to establish a real connection with someone else. I've always been suspicious about ulterior motives. Maybe too suspicious. I never let people get too close—I always ended things before they got serious. Now, with my powers, people are afraid of me, and they have good reason to be. I've got a pretty low risk of cracking, but it's not impossible. So now, dating is even harder, but I've never been good at being single."

"So I'm convenient."

"That's not—"

I put a finger over his lips. "It's okay. Convenient makes sense. There are worse reasons to start a relationship. Not that I'm agreeing to a relationship. But I will take you as my date to my sister's wedding."

"Well, I'll just have to be at my most charming to make sure I get a second date." He glanced up at my alarm clock. "We're late for training. The kids are probably about ready to send out a search party. I'll go assure them that you're okay, just still a bit run down from yesterday. You can take the day off."

"A day off? What exactly am I supposed to do with myself if I'm not training?"

He shrugged. "We have cable."

30

●○●

Dr. Sherman knocked on my door at lunchtime. "I hear you're taking the day off."

"Yeah, Jeff said it was okay."

"Of course it's okay. Do you mind if I come in?" She held out an Arby's bag and a six pack of cheap beer. "I brought bribes."

My stomach rumbled. "Okay."

Dr. Sherman handed me a roast beef sandwich and a beer.

"I could have handled the invitation thing better," she said. "I just knew it was going to upset you and wanted to help. But I'm sure it came across as pushy."

I shrugged. "That's your job, I suppose."

"I know that the team isn't very fond of me," she said.

I choked on my beer. "I'm sure that's not true."

She shrugged. "It's not my job to be liked. But it does get lonely."

"I can see that."

"You faced some pretty serious stress right after waking up with powers, and you're handling it incredibly well. Based on that, my assessment is that you're stable. Unlikely to crack. I will, of course, still have to monitor you. That's my job. But I was hoping that maybe we could be friends, too." She crumpled up a sandwich wrapper and tossed it back into the bag. "I'm tired of not having any friends."

It made sense. If Jeff had been lonely, even as part of the team, Dr. Sherman would be even lonelier.

It wouldn't hurt to give her a chance. "Do you promise not to read my mind without permission?"

She held up three fingers. "Scout's honor."

"So," I said, picking up the TV remote, "we apparently get HBO, and I'm super behind on some shows. You want to watch something?"

●○●

Tabitha came up after dinner to check me over. Halfway through her scan, she stopped and scowled at my knees. "What did you do?"

31

"I may have fallen on them."

"You need to be more careful."

"Tabitha, they're just bruises."

"They're bruises that you can't feel."

"I got my invitation to my sister's wedding this morning."

She looked up at me. "You okay?"

I shrugged. "I'm taking Jeff as my date."

"Good. Me and Teresa can take you dress shopping."

"Okay."

Her eyebrows rose. "Okay? You're just agreeing without any argument?"

"I'm going to need all the help I can get, since I need to outshine the bride without looking like I'm trying to."

Tabitha grinned. "Damn straight." She looked back to my knees. "There isn't any swelling, so they probably are okay. But promise me you'll be more careful."

"I promise."

●○●

Dr. Sherman knocked on my door before breakfast. "I have exciting news! You've been invited to join one of the elite teams! They travel around the world, dealing with natural disasters and facing the worst supervillains. And they have a telekinetic member who could teach you everything he knows."

"I didn't even elite teams were a thing," I said.

"We really should brief you on everything you missed. But now isn't the time. You've been invited to join one of the most high-profile teams on the planet! They actually do fight evil! You'll be able to do work that really matters."

"Oh. That's... cool. But why do they want me?"

"I may have pulled some strings for you—I've been thinking about your mission statement, and this is the best way to accomplish it. And you'd actually be able to train with someone who shares your power set! The local teams do important work, but the elite teams are the ones who are out there saving the world."

I did like the sound of saving the world. But I didn't want to leave my team. Not right after we'd really started to bond. "Can I

32

think about it?" I asked. "My life has been a whirlwind lately, I'm not sure if I'm ready for another big change."

Dr. Sherman sighed. "Andromeda, you can't pass this up because of a crush."

I gaped at her. "A crush?"

"It's clear that you're infatuated with Jeff—and I don't blame you, he's a very attractive man. But there are plenty of other attractive men on the elite team."

"I don't want to stay because of Jeff."

Dr. Sherman rolled her eyes. "Just keep telling yourself that, Andromeda. I'll see if they can wait a few days for you to make up your mind."

● ○ ●

Teresa and Tabitha had very different ideas of how I should eclipse my sister. Teresa's favorite was slinky and red and made me look like a hooker. Tabitha loved a 20's inspired beige sheath dress that was the same color as the walls in the apartment I'd rented with Conner.

Tabitha zipped me into a floaty chiffon gown while Teresa organized things I'd already tried on into "no"s and "maybe"s.

"So, why haven't you asked exactly what happened while you were out?" Teresa asked. "I'd be dying to know everything."

I examined the dress and frowned. It wasn't quite right. "Would knowing make my life any better? Would it make me a better hero or a better person?"

"Probably not," Tabitha said.

"I can't do anything to change the past. I don't want to spend my time looking backwards."

"I'd still want to know," Teresa said.

"Well, she doesn't, so let it go," Tabitha said. "What exactly are you looking for in a dress, Andromeda?"

"I want something that billows when I move." I hung the chiffon dress on the no rack. "In blue. Or maybe purple."

The girls exchanged a grin. "We'll see what we can find."

• ○ •

"You're not going to go, are you?" Dr. Sherman asked. At least this time she brought coffee when she knocked before any rational person would want company.

"It's not that I don't appreciate you doing this for me. I do. But I just want to take some time to get used to the new normal."

Dr. Sherman gave me a skeptical look. "Uh huh."

"I'm not staying for Jeff. Or not just for Jeff. I want to stay for the whole team."

"Even if it means not getting the chance to save the world?"

"Well, if they need me, they know where I am."

• ○ •

I RSVP'd to Cassie and Conner's wedding, and I checked the box that I'd be bringing a plus one. We both opted for the steak dinner. I finally got my first paycheck from the team, and spent it on things to make my room feel a little more personalized. I got one of those sunrise alarm clocks that Conner never wanted to try and I splurged on a pretty watercolor painting of a tree in the snow.

Dr. Sherman and I powered through three seasons of my favorite show, and she started insisting that I call her Viv.

Moving around with my power seemed to be enough to help the muscles that had started to atrophy when I was in my coma, and I started to look healthier when I looked into the mirror. Tabitha printed out stacks of articles about paralysis for me, but lots of them contained conflicting information.

I didn't mention anything about it to Viv—I figured she'd let me know if she finally found a doctor willing to talk to me.

I trained with the team, and I was careful not to overdo it. We helped out with four more fires.

And I got my costume, finally. It was form-fitting Kevlar with ceramic plates for additional protection. Yellow piping ran down the sleeves and legs and up to the collar, but the rest was solid navy.

I tried it out during training, and it felt good to suit up with my team.

"How often do we see action?" I asked during one of Jeff's mandated water breaks. "Are we due for some super villain fights?"

Jeff shrugged. "We mostly fight natural disasters, honestly. The number of new villains has been pretty low for a while. Most people got their powers during the initial emergence. New people do get powers sometimes, but it's not as intense as having so many at the same time."

"So, we're essentially glorified firefighters?"

Landen grinned. "I'm very good at getting cats out of trees."

"The protesters are mad that we're putting normal firefighters out of jobs," Jackson said, rolling his eyes.

"The protestors are mad about a lot of things," Jeff said.

Everyone's phone started chiming. Teresa got to hers first. "Well, that's weirdly timed. We have a 642."

"What is that?" I asked.

"A new super villain," Tabitha said. "Let's go test out your suit."

• ○ •

"Do we have any info on the villain?" I asked as we piled into a nondescript van. Excitement and nerves tugged me in opposite directions, leaving me feeling unexpectedly calm and focused. But then, this is what we'd trained for.

Jeff checked his mirrors. "Everyone strap in."

"I still can't believe we don't have a driver," I muttered as I fastened my seatbelt. "Or a helicopter."

"I'm a very safe driver." Jeff signaled his turn out of the parking lot.

I rolled my eyes. "Info on our bad guy?"

Jackson poked at his phone. "We don't have much. It seems like maybe he has earthquake powers? There are some reports of unusual seismic activity downtown."

"He's holed up in a warehouse," Teresa said. "He was at work when his abilities emerged, and he cracked."

"I really need to get Viv to get me a phone," I said.

"It is odd that you haven't been provided with one yet," Tabitha said. "Your uniform took a while, too. I wonder why."

"Bureaucracy is slow," Landen said. "What's really weird is calling her Viv."

"None of that matters at the moment," Jeff said. "Right now, we need a plan to take this guy out."

"You go in and punch him," I suggested.

Teresa grinned. "Straightforward. I like it."

"He probably has hostages," Jackson said. "Since he just got his powers, it's likely that he doesn't have a solid grasp on how they work. We should utilize that. He shakes things. Do you think you could hold them steady, Andromeda?"

I reminded myself that I could push a tank. "I can give it a try."

The car started shuddering as we approached our destination. The ground around the warehouse was shaking, and cracks spider-webbed the pavement in the parking lot. The warehouse itself, a low, long building covered with gray aluminum siding, looked like an unbalanced washer with an over-enthusiastic spin cycle. Jackson and I floated a few inches off of the ground while the other stumbled out of the car.

"Try stabilizing us," Jeff said.

I reached out with my mind. I couldn't get a grip on the ground—it was too big for me to hold. Instead, I just picked everyone up. "I'm not sure if I can oppose him directly, but I can do this much."

Jeff took a deep breath. I felt his chest expand with my power. "You guys ready to head in?"

"What's this guy's name?" I asked, thinking about how I felt when I first saw Cassandra and Conner.

Jackson glanced at his phone. "Terrence O'Reily. Why?"

"It could have happened to any one of us. We should at least know his name." The others nodded, all suddenly solemn.

I pushed us toward the building, giving Jeff a solid lead.

Inside, the structure was starting to come apart. Cracks ran from the floor to the ceiling, and shattered light fixtures littered the ground. Shelves covered with what looked like car parts were scattered around, and bits of bent and broken metal rattled around our feet. I could feel the vibrations in the air, now, and did my best to shield my team from the pummeling.

Terrence O'Reily stood in a tiny island of stillness, surrounded by shaking rubble and battered corpses. Tears streamed down his face. "I can't make it stop," he said.

"What do we do?" I asked. My voice sounded strange and hollow in the vibrating air.

"You have to kill me," Terrence said. "Please."

"Jesus, Terrence," Teresa said. "It was hard when I got my powers, too. I burned our house down. But you can stop it."

"I can't!" Terrence shouted. "Every time I try, it just gets worse!" The shaking intensified, and what looks like a car engine toppled toward us. I pushed it away, and my grip on everyone else slipped for a second.

Everyone except Jeff cried out in pain.

I caught them again, steadied them. Buffered out the pummeling vibrations. "I don't know how long I can keep this up," I said.

"Take the kids and get out of here," Jeff said.

"No!" Teresa reached toward Terrence. "You don't have to do this. You can learn to control it!"

"Look around, kid. I killed people."

"I did, too," Teresa said. "You can get through this, Terrence."

"Andromeda." Jeff looked at me. "I'm the team leader. Go."

I went. Teresa fought me, but the others were quiet.

As we left the warehouse, the shaking stopped, and I let them go. I hovered over to the van, then sank slowly to the ground.

"We have to go back in there!" Teresa shouted.

I wasn't sure I could carry anyone back in, even if I wanted to. "If Jeff says he's got this, he's got this. I trust him."

"Do you? Or would we still be in there if I was a hot tennis player?"

"I won't stop you from going back in. But I also won't protect you," I said. Which was a lie, if she ran back in I would do anything I could to keep her safe. Even if all I could manage at the moment was to clutch at her ankles.

She glared at me, then stalked away from the building.

I leaned against the van, let it support most of my weight.

Tabitha came up and stood beside me. "Did you overdo it again?"

"Yeah. I'm okay, but I need a break."

A few minutes later, Jeff came out of the broken building carrying Terrence's body.

"Is he dead?" Teresa asked.

Jeff shook his head. "I just knocked him out. I wasn't sure if that would work. I'm glad it did."

"Do you think we'll be able to help him?" Jackson asked.

Landen patted Jackson's shoulder. "If anyone can help him, it's us."

I thought about the look in Terrence's eyes, about the broken bodies of his coworkers at his feet. I wasn't sure if Terrence O'Reily would appreciate our help.

•○•

Tabitha was quiet as she looked me over.

"Is Teresa okay?" I asked.

"She will be. She's strong."

"Can I ask what happened? When you two got your powers?"

"Teresa was home with our parents. I was out. I wanted to be near the ocean—I could feel the water's pull, at that point. Our powers emerged at the same moment. I was standing on the beach under the moon, feeling the power of the water all around me. She was at home, and the pilot light in the oven went crazy."

"I'm so sorry."

Tabitha checked one foot, then the other. "I'm just glad she didn't crack. That I didn't lose all of them." She looked up and met my eyes. "You look okay. Good job. And thanks for protecting us in there. You were great. And for what it's worth, I think you were right to trust Jeff."

"Thanks, Tabitha. I'll see you tomorrow."

She hugged me, and even though I couldn't feel most of it, it felt right.

•○•

Teresa knocked on my door in the middle of the night, jerking me out of a dream where Terrence O'Reily was trapped in a snow globe that was slowly cracking into pieces.

"I'm sorry I was a jerk, you kept us all alive tonight."

We sat together on my bed. "You know, I would have still tried to protect you if you went back in."

"I should have known that Jeff would try to take him down without killing him. Jeff is a good guy. And you two are cute together."

38

"I'm not sure if he's really serious about me, or just lonely," I said.

Teresa shrugged. "If you like him, does it really matter?"

• ○ •

We were all sitting together, eating in silence, when Viv joined us the next morning. I knew that could only mean bad news. She never ate with the team.

"Terrence O'Reily killed himself last night," she said. She reached out and patted Teresa's shoulder, and the girl flinched away from her touch. "You mustn't blame yourselves," Viv continued. "You did all that you could."

"How did he manage it?" Tabitha asked. "I thought he was sedated."

"His power must have impacted his metabolism, somehow. He woke up in the middle of the night and hung himself with the bedsheets."

"But that means he was awake without his powers going crazy," Teresa said.

"It's possible that his power was still suppressed even though he was conscious," Viv said. "I just wanted to let you know before you saw it on the news. I know how badly you wanted to help him."

Tabitha and Teresa gave Viv twin glares as she left.

I fed a piece of toast to Landen's squirrel. "I know she's awkward, but I do think she means well," I said.

Teresa rubbed her shoulder. "I wish she wouldn't touch me."

Landen frowned. "We're required to submit to her scans whenever she asks."

"But she never asks," Teresa snapped.

"Maybe she thinks it would be more awkward if she did ask," Jackson said, reappearing in the chair next to me. He'd gone invisible when Viv walked in.

"Consent is important," I said. "I can mention it to her."

"No, I'll talk to her about it," Jeff said. "As the team leader, it's my responsibility."

Viv flopped down onto my bed. "Jeff thinks that I'm a monster," she said.

"He talked to you about consent?"

She sighed. "I knew that you'd all be upset about Terrence O'Reily. Especially Teresa. I didn't read her. I just put my hand on her shoulder so she'd be focused on being mad at me instead of dwelling on his death."

"You have to stop casting yourself as the bad guy to everyone. There are other ways to make people feel better."

Viv rolled over and buried her face in my pillow. "Jeff also informed me that he was going to be your escort to your sister's wedding."

"Yeah. I mean, he's a more appropriate plus one than Jackson."

"Don't bullshit me, Andromeda. You're falling for him. And who can blame you? He's Jeff Appleton."

She reached out, then paused. "Is it okay if I take your hands? I won't read you."

I nodded, and she grabbed both of my hands between hers. It was still so jarring, seeing someone touch me but not being able to feel it. "There aren't any rules against dating within a team, but it's not encouraged. If things go badly, it could be a serious detriment to the team. As your supervisor, I advise against it."

"What about as my friend?"

Viv sighed. "I don't want you to get your heart broken. And you know his reputation. Breaking hearts is what he does."

I nodded. It was hard to associate the Jeff I knew with his reputation. But maybe he was adorably devoted to everyone he dated, till he got tired of them.

"It's not really my place to talk about it, but you're not the first team member he's dated. He was with a woman named Delania Adams. Laney."

"What happened to her?" I wondered if she'd requested a transfer, or died with all of the other adult heroes.

"They had a fight, and she cracked."

"Oh." Poor Jeff.

"It took the whole team to take her down. I just need you to understand that the danger is real. I'm not just being paranoid. You have to be careful."

"It's just one date," I said.

Viv rolled her eyes. "I don't need to be a mind reader to know that you're full of crap."

• o •

It was frighteningly easy to forget that Jeff, my Jeff, the guy who nagged me to eat breakfast every morning, was Jeff Appleton. When he came to my door the morning of my sister's wedding, wearing a tux and looking every inch a celebrity, the insanity of my current life hit me again.

"Are you sure you want to subject yourself to this?" I asked.

"You look beautiful."

I blushed. "So do you."

He grinned and extended his arm. I took it, wishing I could feel the silk under my fingertips. "I wonder if your tux cost more than my sister's dress."

"Probably. It's handmade." He waited till we were in the elevator to tell me his next surprise. "I also rented us a limo."

"Oh, so today we can have a driver?"

"Well, I can drive a van. I can't drive a limo."

"So, I'm showing up to my sister's wedding with her childhood crush wearing a handmade silk tuxedo in a limo. I wonder if that's over the line or not."

"Her wedding to your former fiancé. I think pulling out all of the stops is only fair."

I didn't argue. I folded myself into the limo's leather interior and looked around. There was a bottle of champagne in a mini fridge and two crystal goblets.

"That's for after," Jeff said. "I'm sure you haven't had anything except coffee so far today, and drinking on an empty stomach is never a good idea."

I rolled my eyes. "Sure, Mom."

"Oh, no, don't you start."

41

"I'm starting to wonder if you've invested heavily in cereal companies or something."

"Of course not. My money is all in waffles."

I stared out the tinted windows as we rolled out of the city.

"Are you okay?" Jeff asked.

"I'm pretty sure Conner never really wanted to marry me. He asked because we'd been together so long. Because staying together was easier than breaking up."

Jeff reached out and traced the edges of my ear. "I'm glad that he missed his shot with you. Because it means that I get one."

"Are you angling for a second date already? This one still has plenty of time to flop."

"Oh, don't even try to pretend that the limo didn't score me any points."

"Maybe a few."

"Enough for a second date? Maybe a movie and dinner someplace with more choices than steak or fish?"

I thought about Viv's warning. I could stop this here, leave it at harmless flirting, not put my heart on the line with a world-famous playboy who was only interested because I as convenient. But I did like him. I really, really liked him. "Okay."

He grinned like a second date with me was the best present he'd ever received. He looked really great in the tux. I leaned my head on his shoulder. He smelled nice, too.

"So, are your parents going to be there?" Jeff asked. "Do I need to worry about making a good impression?"

I shook my head. "They died when I was in college. Cassie is my only family."

"Were the two of you close?"

"We were."

"It's not too late to just skip this, you know. I could take you anywhere."

"I think I need to be there. For me, not for them."

"Okay," Jeff said. "But if you want to bail, just let me know. We can have a secret signal. Like, if you pull on your earlobe, that'll be my cue."

"How about I pull on your earlobe?" I asked, tugging on it with my power to demonstrate.

"Oh, that's better. Yes. Do that. You'd be an excellent spy."

I laughed, and he kept me distracted with stories about the spy movie he'd starred in till the limo stopped.

I was more nervous than I'd been before my first super villain fight. If I wasn't paralyzed, I would have been shaking. The driver opened the door for us, and I floated out.

I hadn't been out of the city since I woke up, and I'd kept busy. I hadn't noticed how much I'd missed being out in nature. The venue was a wildlife center, and the decorations were pretty, but rustic. Jeff and the limo, and even me in my flowing purple dress, all looked a little out of place.

Jeff looked around, and I could tell that he was carefully keeping his face blank.

"How much do you hate the décor?" I asked.

"More than a little," he said.

I didn't hate it, but it certainly wasn't what I would have picked. But then, it wasn't my wedding.

Jeff held out his arm, and I took it. I concentrated on moving my body, one step and then the next. Like I was normal and walking on my feet instead of floating just off of the ground.

I'd mostly stopped pretending to walk at home.

The usher, one of the kids that Conner had met volunteering at Big Brothers Big Sisters, was so busy staring at Jeff that he didn't recognize me. "Bride's side or groom's?"

"Bride's," I said.

Rows of metal folding chairs had been set up in the largest classroom, and classical music was playing from set of portable speakers in the corner. I was pretty sure those had been mine, actually. I stifled the impulse to crush them with my mind.

The usher showed us to our seats. The folding chairs looked uncomfortable, and Jeff was still keeping his face pleasantly blank. He was definitely finding the venue lacking.

When had I learned how to read him so well?

We'd timed it so that we wouldn't be early or late, to maybe try to blend in with the crowd.

But there wasn't much of a crowd, and they were already all staring at us.

I at least recognized most of them. Cassie's friends from high school, Conner's friends from college.

Jeff casually took my hand and laced our fingers together. He leaned close and whispered in my ear, "Remember the signal. We can always claim superhero business and flee."

"I thought it was important for heroes to face their fears," I whispered back.

"You read too many comic books."

I laughed, and I could feel the stares intensifying. If I wanted to, I could turn all of them away from us. I pushed the thought away. I was the one who brought a movie star as my date. I might as well have worn a sign that said, "Please stare at me."

A few more people came in and also stared. They all sat carefully away from us, like we might be contagious.

Then, finally, the ceremony started. Conner and some guy in a green polo and khakis walked up to the front of the room, and some weird, new-agey music started playing.

Jeff, his face oh-so-carefully movie-star blank, put his arm around my shoulder and pulled gently on my earlobe.

I had to disguise my laugh as a coughing fit.

The groomsmen and bridesmaids tried to walk in time to the beat as they proceeded slowly up the aisle.

Just as the music built up to the requisite vaguely ethnic warbling, Cassie appeared in the door.

Her dress was simple. Long and white with an empire waist and modest neckline. She was wearing the diamond necklace and earrings that our grandmother had left to me.

She'd probably decided to wear them as a tribute while I'd been in a coma. And then hadn't thought about finding something else and giving them back to me. Ripping them off of her or choking her with the necklace both would have been bad ideas.

But it would be so terrifyingly easy.

I wondered what cracking actually felt like. If you'd notice when it happened, or if you'd think you were still perfectly sane.

Jeff leaned over and whispered in my ear, "This music is an abomination. How does it keep getting worse?"

I was really glad that I'd brought him with me.

The rest of the ceremony was uneventful. Polo guy's officiating was full of passages that sounded like he'd lifted them from self-help manuals, and everyone's gaze flicked over to me when he asked if anyone had any objections.

I kept my mouth shut.

Cassie and Conner kissed.

I made myself watch without blinking. I ignored the tears that slipped down my cheeks. I felt like something had reached into my chest and torn my heart in half. I could sense every inch of the building, every person sitting inside it.

I could rip them all apart.

But I didn't.

I'd faced it. It was over, and I hadn't gone crazy and killed anyone.

On the way out of the church, Cassie hugged me. "Oh Andi, it means so much that you came," she said, blinking back happy tears. "And I love your hair!"

"Yeah," Conner said. "It's really good to see you."

"Thanks," I said. I couldn't think of another word to say that wouldn't be hurtful.

"It was a lovely ceremony," Jeff said, sounding utterly sincere. "Thank you so much for inviting us."

"Well, technically—" Conner started, and Cassie elbowed him.

"It really does mean a lot that you came," she said again, her voice soft.

"When Andromeda told me that her sister was getting married, I figured it would be a great chance to get to meet her family."

Conner glared at him. "She hates it when people call her Andromeda."

"I actually go by it, now." I said. "It works pretty well as a superhero name." They both winced at the word *superhero*. "Anyway, we should get moving, we're holding up the line." I kissed Cassie on the cheek and hugged Conner, being extremely careful to be gentle. I could feel each breath they took, each heartbeat. I could still crush them, if I wanted.

I didn't.

I floated away, not bothering to pretend to walk.

● ○ ●

We went to the reception, because I'm apparently some kind of masochist. The steaks were rubbery, but the cake was good.

45

The music continued to be terrible, but we were dancing anyway, and Jeff was charming and distracting and altogether an excellent date. I told myself that no matter what else happened between us, I'd always be grateful for this. I wasn't sure I would have made it through without him.

I could still sense everything around me, and I could shake the whole building as easily as I was shaking my money maker.

That's why I noticed when someone shot a blow dart at me from the bushes.

If my power hadn't still been emotionally supercharged, it would have hit me and I wouldn't have noticed. But I felt it slicing through the air at me, and I caught it. I just held it for an instant, feeling out its shape and purpose. Then I felt a second one, and caught that, too.

I reached out with my power, to the hedges around the venue, then tree trunks and ferns, and there was a person, a woman, holding a long, thin pipe. I crushed the pipe and pinned her to the ground. I muffled the vibration of her shouts and stuffed my power into her mouth like a gag.

"Are you okay?" Jeff asked. "You look distracted."

"Someone in the bushes just shot these at me. I've got her pinned, but I'm not sure what else to do with her," I said, floating the darts to Jeff, careful to keep the gleaming tip away from him. "Be careful with these, I'm sure they're poisoned."

His eyes widened in alarm. He grabbed a burlap napkin from one of the tables and wrapped the darts in it. "I'll get them tested when we get back home. And I can make a call and a cleanup team to come take the perp in. Will you be okay without me for a few minutes?"

I nodded, and he ducked around a corner.

Questioning bad guys wasn't my job. I didn't have any training for it. But someone had been targeting me, and I wanted to know why. So, as soon as Jeff was out of sight, I turned to float over.

But my sister was hurrying toward me, her train pinned up in the back and her shoes left behind somewhere. She crossed her arms over her chest. "I've been trying to get you alone," she said.

I was very aware of the stranger in the bushes. She wriggled against my hold, but it didn't do her any good.

"Why?" I asked.

"I know that Jeff Appleton is insanely hot, and it's cool that you are on a super team together, but dating him is a bad idea. I've been his fan for a long time, I know how he is. He's a heartbreaker, Andi."

"Andromeda. I go by Andromeda now. Andi's dead. Gone with her relationships and all of her stuff, apparently." I flicked the earrings with my mind.

Cassi cupped her hands over the earrings, like that could protect them from me. "What are you talking about?"

"They told me that you gave away everything I owned. Was seeing it too much of a reminder that I'd ever existed?"

"We didn't give away your things. They're in storage. They told us that you didn't want them. And I tried calling you about five hundred times."

"I don't have a phone," I said.

"They gave me a number. I would have come in person, but we were told that you needed space, that we should wait for you to come to us."

"Who told you that?" I asked.

"That Dr. Sherman lady told me to wait till you contacted me. The rest was all in form letters."

I could definitely imagine Viv telling them to give me space. But I had no idea who had screwed up the communication about my stuff. I really did need to get a phone.

"I'm sorry, Andi—Andromeda. I'm sorry that I gave up on you waking up. That I fell in love with Conner. That I didn't try harder to see you again after you woke up. I can't even imagine how you feel about all of this. I wouldn't have blamed you if you'd never wanted to see either of us again." Tears shone in her eyes. She really was very pretty in her wedding dress.

I really wanted to stay mad at her, but I'd always been weak to her tears. I loved her, after all.

And hearing that I might be able to get my possessions back was a relief. "Why didn't you lead with that?"

That startled a pained laugh out of her, and she wiped her cheeks with the backs of her hands. "I'm still your big sister."

"You've hurt me worse than Jeff ever could."

She sagged. "I know I have. But that doesn't mean I want you to get hurt again."

"Jeff and the rest of my team are the best thing in my life right now, Cassie. They're what get me out of bed every morning."

"Just promise me that you'll be careful," Cassie said. "Don't fall in love with him too fast. I'm worried—" she broke off, then took a deep breath. "I'm worried that if someone else breaks your heart, you might crack."

I fought not to wince. "I'll take it under advisement. Now, you'd better get back in there."

"Are we okay?" she asked.

"Oh, Cassie. No. But I hope we will be, someday."

"Can I—Can I hug you?"

"I won't feel it."

She stepped forward, arms outstretched. "That wasn't a no."

I let her hug me. And I didn't even think about the fact that I could turn her inside out with my brain.

It wasn't healing, yet. But it was progress.

I figured that Jeff would be back any second, but I floated over to my would-be-assailant anyway. The bushes blocked the view, so no other wedding guests could see us.

I don't know why I wasn't prepared to see the pure hatred in her eyes. She had attacked me, after all. I recognized her— the blonde protestor with the egg from the Protectors of the Mundane rally.

"What was on the darts?" I asked, releasing my hold on her mouth so that she could answer.

"You'll see, sooner or later," she snarled. "And then the whole world will see that you're all monsters."

●○●

The next morning, Jeff called the team to the cafeteria and we all sat in silence while he paced. "The news isn't good," he said after a solid three minutes.

"Well, that's a surprise," Teresa said, sarcasm coating every syllable.

"There's a long scientific explanation as to how, but the substance on the darts—it makes people lose control of their powers."

"Is that what happened to Terrence O'Reily?" Tabitha asked. "Did someone shoot him with one of those darts?"

"There's no way to prove it at this point, but it seems likely."

"Who would do something like that?" Jackson asked. "And why?"

"The Protectors of the Mundane," I said. "And to keep people afraid of us. With fewer new people emerging, fewer people are cracking. So they've found a way to crack us artificially."

"Innocent people died in that warehouse," Landen said.

"People would have died yesterday if Andromeda had lost it, too," Teresa added. "Any one of us could hurt people."

I remembered Terrence O'Reily's face, and thought about what would have happened if one of those darts had hit me yesterday. "It would have looked like I cracked under the pressure from the wedding," I said. "No one would have suspected a thing."

"We don't know how widespread this is," Jeff said. "I've passed the info along to the other teams, so they'll know to be careful."

"We can't let this stand," Teresa said. "We need to shut them down."

"That's not our job," Jeff said.

"No, our job is sitting here doing nothing," Teresa snapped.

Tabitha put a hand on her sister's shoulder. "We're not above the law."

"We should leave this to the non-powered authorizes," Jeff said. "We could very easily be liabilities instead of assets."

"Jeff, Landen, and I would be the best off," Jackson said. "Things could go really bad if they got any of the girls, though."

"Have you seen *The Birds*?" Landen asked. "I'm pretty sure I could do some damage, too."

"Is that a movie?" Jackson asked.

Landen buried his face in his hands. "Jesus, yes. It's a movie. Did you grow up in a cave?"

"It is pretty old," Tabitha said.

"I own it, we're watching it after training."

"A movie night sounds good," I said. I was glad that the conversation had turned away from the poison and the Protectors of the Mundane. Obsessing about it wasn't going to do any of us any good. Even though I couldn't get the look on that woman's face out of my mind.

I grabbed myself a cup of coffee while the kids moved on to squabbling about what kind of dinner we should order. Jeff joined me. For once, he didn't even glance at the food.

"Are our uniforms dart-proof?" I asked.

"I'll make sure of it," he said. "And I'll see if we can get redesigns that cover as much skin as possible."

I nodded. "Good idea." I put a hand on his shoulder. Even though I couldn't feel it, he could. "I think they took it well."

"They're a resilient bunch."

"How are you holding up?"

"I keep imagining how things could have gone yesterday. It's going to be giving me nightmares for a while." He stared into his coffee. "We got lucky."

I squeezed his shoulder. "And now that we know what we're up against, we can be careful."

"Right."

"Now, are you going to have some breakfast?" I asked. "We don't want you crashing at 10am."

He took my hand from his shoulder and kissed my palm, and I wanted more than anything to be able to feel his lips against my skin. "I'll make us both omelets."

● ○ ●

Movie night was going really well. We had a projector set up in the big common room, and there was more than enough couch space for all of us. I was sitting with my feet in Jeff's lap, and the kids kept glancing over, smiling, and exchanging knowing looks.

Then Viv came in with a very carefully impassive look on her face. One that could only mean bad news. She cleared her throat, and Landen paused the movie.

"I hate to always be the bearer of bad news, but you're all restricted to the tower unless on a mission for the foreseeable future," she said. She twisted her fingers together, her knuckles white. "The decision was made at the highest levels, and is going to be enforced throughout the country. Possibly throughout the world."

"That's absurd," Jeff said. "They can't just treat us like criminals."

"I am sorry," said Viv.

"Are you not allowed to leave, too?" I asked.

"We're all under house arrest," Viv said.

"Whatever," Teresa said. "I can't blame them for being scared." Her calm acceptance was worrying. I tried to catch Tabitha's eye, but she was still looking toward the screen.

"This is a violation of our basic rights," Jeff said. "We can't just shrug it off."

"We don't have a choice," Viv said.

"I'm going to go call my lawyers," Jeff said.

"Do you want us to wait for you to get back?" Landen asked.

"Nah, go ahead. I've seen it."

After a few moments of awkward hovering, Viv followed him out. Landen started the movie back up, and we watched in silence.

●○●

Jeff's lawyers made him vague promises that they'd do what they could, but that appeared to be a lot of nothing.

"I don't know why he's so upset about this," Tabitha said one evening as she was scanning me for bruises. "It's not like we ever went out much anyway. I'd rather just stay here with you guys between missions. Why risk going out when there are people out there who want to not just kill us, but use us to kill other people, too?"

"It's not really about going out," I said. "It's about personal freedom. Who has it, and who doesn't. Once we let it go, it's gone."

Tabitha pursed her lips and motioned for me to turn around. "Well, I guess that's as good of a use for his rich white guy privilege as any. But I don't know if there's going to be a way to keep supers from being second class citizens. No matter how much good we do, they're always going to be scared of us. I think they might have been scared of us even without the cracking."

I remembered Cassie warning me to keep Jeff at arm's length, her fear of me cracking. Just how bad had things been, right after

51

the emergence? It would be easy to find out, but I'd done my best not to look into anything that happened while I was out. I thought about just how small the crowd had been at Cassie's wedding. About how much trouble Viv was having finding me a doctor. About how, looking back, none of the stores I'd gone into with Jeff were crowded.

I could ask Tabitha. She'd tell me. But I just couldn't see how knowing would matter. Instead, I asked something else. "If you feel that way, why be a superhero? Why dedicate your life to helping people?"

"People don't need to be perfect, or even good, to deserve saving."

● ○ ●

"So, it looks like we won't be going out for that second date," Jeff said. "But I thought maybe we could order in?" He had the menu for an absurd French place pulled up on his tablet. "We can get it delivered."

I kissed him on the cheek, lightly, like it wasn't the start of something huge. He smelled nice, and he was solid and real and warm.

He blushed, and we stood there grinning at each other like giddy teenagers.

"Oh god, parents, get a room," Teresa said as she walked by. But she was grinning, too.

● ○ ●

Teresa seemed to have a thing about coming to my room in the middle of the damn night. "The Protectors of the Mundane targeted you personally," she said, walking in and sitting down on my bed.

I blinked groggily at her. "It's 3am."

"I want to take the fight to them. I don't want to wait for them to figure out how to aerosolize their stupid poison."

I sat up. "What's your plan?"

"Well, they have a headquarters, I figured I'd burn it down."

52

I buried my face in both hands. "That is the worst plan that I've ever heard."

"Do you have a better one?"

"We could send Jackson in to spy and see if he can get proof that they're behind the attack."

"That's a good idea," Jackson said, appearing next to the door.

"Holy crap, how often are you lurking about invisible?" Teresa asked.

Jackson shrugged. "How often do you have secret meetings at 3am?"

"Are you able to sneak out of here?" I asked. I could only trust that Jackson didn't actually make a habit of sneaking into my room.

"Easily."

Teresa scowled. "I don't like that I have nothing to do in this plan."

"What are you talking about?" Jackson said. "You're going to have to cover for me. If anyone figures out that I'm gone, I could get in serious trouble."

Teresa sighed. "That's not nearly as satisfying as burning their building down."

"Maybe not," I said. "But being a hero isn't always about what's most satisfying for us."

Teresa sighed. "Fine. When do we want to do this?"

● ○ ●

Being under house arrest hadn't really changed our routine. Jeff had been the only one who went out much.

He and I took turns picking movies for our date nights. He preferred weird artsy stuff that I found myself liking more than I expected. I made him watch all of the horror classics that he'd somehow missed.

It was my job to distract him while Teresa kept Landen and Tabitha occupied and Jackson snuck out to spy.

Part of me wanted to just tell Jeff, but I wasn't sure how he'd react to the plan. So I picked a long, complicated movie and put my head on his shoulder.

I tried not to worry about Jackson. He was just a kid, but he could handle this.

Jeff headed to his room around 11. Teresa knocked on my door around 1. "Landen and Tabitha are asleep."

I nodded. "You should get some rest, too."

She snorted and sat down on my bed. I floated back and forth, and wondered if pacing had actually been more soothing when I could feel my feet.

It was nearly dawn when my door opened then closed again. Jackson appeared, leaning against it. "As far as I can tell, they don't have any intel on the poison at all. I searched for hours. There's no sign of any kind of lab, no place that they're storing any kind of chemicals. I managed to see a few executives' passwords, and I didn't even find any reference to it in their emails and files. It looks like all they do is lobby and organize protests."

"You didn't find any hint of any illegal activity?" Teresa asked.

"Well, there was some shady money stuff happening. But nothing like what I was looking for."

"That means that the woman who tried to poison me got it from a different source."

"What happened to her?" Teresa asked. "Maybe we could ask her some questions."

"I'll look into it," I said.

●○●

Viv and I caught up on my favorite show and we were starting in on her favorite, a British period romance with lots of pining and longing glances and forbidden love.

It wasn't the kind of thing I'd pick up on my own, but it was fairly compelling.

"So, whatever happened to that woman who tried to poison me?"

Viv shifted uncomfortably. "Oh, didn't I tell you?"

"I think we all just assumed she was arrested."

"Well, she was. And they were all set to detain her and question her." Viv pinched the bridge of her nose. "Apparently she had a false tooth filled with cyanide."

54

"She killed herself?"

"It was a suicide mission from the start. She had to know that if you lost control of your power she'd be ripped apart. The cyanide tooth must have been insurance that no one would be able to question her." Viv shook her head. "I had no idea that the Protectors of the Mundane were so fanatical."

I wanted to point out that they weren't, but I couldn't tell Viv how I knew that.

Either way, it was a dead end.

• ○ •

There was a quiet knock on my door before breakfast, and Tabitha handed me a cup of coffee when I let her in. "Do you have some time to talk?" she said.

"Of course."

"I can't stop thinking about that poison. I just keep wondering why anyone would want to create something so horrible. It exists to hurt people. It doesn't have any other purpose. Most poisons do actually have some medicinal use, in the right hands. But not this. It's just... evil."

She reached toward my bathroom, and a head-sized globe of water oozed from the faucet and floated toward us. It split into two smaller spheres, then split again. "I've never lost control of my power," she said. "From the moment it emerged, it's just felt like a natural part of me. I love it. I don't want it to be something that I'm afraid of."

I couldn't think of anything to say that wouldn't be an empty platitude. So I just nodded.

The globes kept splitting, till hundreds of tiny spheres of water surrounded us, glinting in the light. Tabitha's forehead furrowed with concentration.

"If we ever do water balloons, I want to be on your team," I said.

Tabitha snorted, and the globes burst, soaking us both.

And then we were both giggling, and for at least a second, things were okay.

55

●○●

I started exchanging letters with my sister. She sent me some boxes and I cried over my battered paperback copy of *Bridge to Terabithia.*

Tabitha kept checking me for bruises, and she, Teresa, and I got subscription boxes for a bunch of random superhero-themed crap that we shared between the three of us. My room was slowly filling up.

We spent time training as a team, and we had weekly movie and pizza nights.

After a couple of quiet weeks, Jackson, Teresa, and I decided to tell Jeff what we knew about the Protectors of the Mundane.

They agreed that I should be the one to break the news.

Jeff and I were eating the best Chinese food I'd ever had, and he was watching me with this tiny smile that I really liked putting on his face. I was levitating the food straight into my mouth, carefully crafting perfectly balanced bites of meat, vegetables, and rice with my mind.

"I really want to kiss you," he said, and I choked.

He was polite enough to ignore my hacking as I struggled with my water.

"I'd be okay with that," I finally managed. We'd been moving slowly, not really talking about what our dates meant.

He brushed a stray hair back behind my ear, and kissed me.

I wasn't sure if I'd forgotten what it was like, or if he was just a much better kisser than Conner.

I pulled away and took a deep breath. "I have something that I have to tell you."

●○●

"Jackson did what?" Jeff shouted. "Of all of the idiotic—dangerous—stupid—he's a child, Andromeda!"

"He's a superhero! And we had to do something!"

"But you didn't do anything! You sat back and sent our team's youngest member into what you thought was the most dangerous place on the goddamn planet! What if they had been aerosolizing

56

the poison? What if they'd caught him? Being invisible doesn't make him invulnerable! He still shows up on thermal scans!"

"If he hadn't gone, we wouldn't have been able to talk Teresa out of doing something rash."

"Talking her out of things isn't your job, it's mine. You should have come to me with this, Andromeda. I'm the team leader."

"I couldn't just rat them out! They trusted me!"

"So did I!"

"I'm sorry that I hid this from you. But it's important intel, and we needed it. We can't just wait for your lawyers. Whoever the government has looking into this—they're looking in the wrong place. The Protectors of the Mundane didn't make the poison. I assumed that whoever did would make another move, give us another lead. But they haven't. They could be planning something big."

Jeff rubbed his temples. "I'll do what I can to get the info the right people without implicating Teresa and Jackson. But you're suspended. When we go out on missions, you'll stay here. You're going to have to earn my trust back."

He slammed the door on his way out. I gathered up takeout containers and tried not to cry.

●○●

The next morning, Jeff didn't make me an omelet.

I ripped a piece of toast into tiny pieces and drank coffee. "Andromeda won't be training with us today," Jeff said.

"What? Why?" Tabitha asked.

"She needs to take some time to think about what the concept of being on a team means." He slid a tablet toward me without looking in my direction. "I've got some assigned reading on there for you."

"This is bullshit," Teresa said.

Jackson stood up. "You can't just punish her for something she didn't do alone. Maybe you're the one who needs to think about what being on a team means."

"What is going on?" Landen asked.

Teresa crossed her arms over her chest. "Andromeda and I sent Jackson to gather intel in the Protectors of the Mundane's HQ."

"No one sent me, it was my idea," Jackson said. "Andromeda and Teresa just covered for me. If you're going to punish someone, it should be me."

"Why didn't you tell us?" Tabitha asked. "You know we have your back."

Teresa sighed. "You're right. We should have told you. But we didn't want the whole team to get in trouble if we got caught."

"You're my responsibility," Jeff said. "If I don't know what you're doing, that is on me. I've apparently been distracted lately. That ends now."

Tabitha looked from Jeff to me, then back to Jeff. "Look, I'm hurt that they hid this, too. But we're still a team. We have to learn from our mistakes, not let them break us."

"Enough," Jeff snapped. "It's time to train. Andromeda, you're to go to your quarters and read."

I picked up the tablet. "Understood."

Jackson's hands clenched into fists, but I caught his eye and shook my head.

The team went to train, and I went upstairs to read.

• o •

I tried to stick with the assigned readings, but they were dry and just made me angry. So instead, I started shelving the box of books that Cassie had sent. I only got halfway through before I started reading one of those instead.

Landen knocked on my door while I was in the middle of *The Shining*, and I tried to not look guilty or surprised that he was standing in my doorway. "Hey," I said. "What's up?"

He shifted his weight back and forth, opened his mouth, then closed it again. Then his eyes fell on my book, and the next thing I knew we were kneeling next to my bookshelf, comparing favorites, and he had an armful of books that he'd never read before.

"So, did you come here to talk about books?" I asked as he read the back of one.

His mouth quirked in a sardonic smile. "No, I came to ask for advice."

"About what?"

58

He took a deep breath. "There's this guy I like. We've been texting."

"Landen, my relationship literally just blew up this morning."

He shrugged. "Who else am I going to ask? Teresa would make fun, Tabitha would tell me he was flirting even if he wasn't. Jackson would have even less of an idea than I do. And Jeff would try to tell me how to flirt back." He shuddered.

"I'm not sure that I'll be able to help either. But I guess I can try."

"Thanks, Andromeda." He pulled his phone out of his pocket. "I'm not sure if he is flirting with me or not. Would you look and tell me what you think?"

I took the phone and started scrolling through the messages. The conversation was painfully sweet. I was really glad I wasn't diabetic. "I think he's interested," I said.

"You do?"

"Landen, there are a lot of heart emojis here."

"And you think that means he likes me?"

I nodded and handed his phone back.

"He's a hero, too."

I'd put that together—they'd been commiserating on the house arrest situation. "That's good—you two have that in common to talk about."

He nodded. "He's also really cute."

"Well, that's good."

"I was thinking about setting up a video call and watching a movie together. Do you think he'd go for it?"

"He'd be crazy not to."

Landen grinned. Then he snagged another book from my shelf. "Oh, can I borrow this too? We should form a book club. Jackson has this super weird collection of Japanese horror manga."

"Oh man, I have to see those."

"Tabitha reads a whole bunch of nonfiction, and Teresa is into these weird romance things. I bet we could all expand each other's literary horizons."

He didn't mention Jeff, and I could help but feel grateful for that.

By the time I went to bed, I had a whole stack of manga to read. I didn't get much sleep.

But it was better than moping over getting dumped.

As the sun was coming up, I sent an ebook copy of the first book in the creepy manga series to Conner.

He hated horror, and he swore at me for giving him nightmares. But it was nice to be talking again.

•○•

"So, I still don't have a phone," I said.

Viv frowned, "I'll reach out about it again."

"Thanks."

"So," she said. "How are things with you and Jeff?"

"He dumped me."

"I can't help but be relieved, honestly." A small, pleased smile tugged at the corners of her mouth. "I'm sorry that it didn't work out." She started picking at the label on her beer bottle. "You have to admit that it's probably for the best, though."

I shrugged. I was still trying not to think about it.

"I had been wondering..." she trailed off.

"Wondering what?"

"How were you two going to deal with sex?"

I hadn't even thought about sex. We'd only even kissed once. But Jeff wasn't paralyzed from the neck down. And I didn't even know what I could or couldn't do anymore. How could I overlook something so basic? "That's a good question," I said.

"Did you not even talk about it?"

I shook my head.

"Hmm."

"What?"

"Well, that doesn't seem like a good sign. I mean, Jeff's a healthy man in his prime, after all. And he does have a certain reputation."

"He didn't give me any reason to doubt him," I said. But would he really have been okay with things continuing on like they had? Maybe he'd been looking for an excuse to end things.

Viv shrugged. "He is an actor. We can assume that he's a really great liar."

The idea that our entire relationship might have been a lie hurt. "Maybe you're right," I said. "Maybe it was for the best."

"Do you want me to reach out to see if there's still a slot on the elite team?"

I shook my head. "I really didn't just stay for Jeff."

●○●

A few days later, Jeff came to my room and gave me a test on the assigned reading. And because I was a mature, functional adult, I did not ram the paper down his throat. I did shred it into a thousand tiny pieces, though.

He pushed into my room and slammed the door behind him. "Acting like a child isn't going to help you earn your way back onto the team."

I glared at him. "If I'm acting like a child, it's because you're treating me like one. You can't have it both ways. You can't punish just me and then pretend that you're being rational. You're angry with me. Fine, I understand. I hurt you, and I'm sorry. You broke up with me. You can't keep me off of the team, too."

"I didn't break up with you," Jeff said.

"Because we weren't really together in the first place?" That really hurt. Enough that I could feel the room around us.

"No. We're still together."

"But you—"

"I'm angry. You did hurt me. I thought you trusted me, and I don't like that I was wrong. But that doesn't mean I don't care about you anymore. We can be fighting and still be together."

"That was not clear to me," I said. "None of this relationship has been clear to me. I still don't know why you even want to be with me."

"Andromeda—"

"You stormed out of my room. You suspended me from the team and sent me to my room to think about what I'd done. You haven't looked at me for days."

"I didn't—"

"You're the team leader. You're the megastar. You're the one calling all of the shots. If we're together, we should be partners. Equals. Maybe I should have trusted you, but if I'd come to you

61

with our plan, would you have trusted me? Would you have let us go ahead, or would you have stopped us?"

Jeff stepped toward me, then stopped. "I can't help being the team leader or a megastar. I don't know how to convince you that I actually care about you, that I do see you as an equal."

"Well, you could start by treating me like one. Put me back on the team."

"The test—"

"I am not taking your stupid test. I'm not sitting out training anymore. You can't stop me." I picked him up with my mind, held him a few inches off of the floor. "I don't like feeling helpless, Jeff. If we're together, I'm vulnerable. Maybe everyone's right. Maybe us being together is a terrible idea."

I dropped him floated toward the door.

"Wait," he said. "Wait, please." He took a deep breath. "God, I'm such a hypocrite. I've been hiding something from you, too."

I scowled at him. "Of course."

He shifted from one foot to the other. "It isn't something I've told many people. And when I have, it's never gone well."

I waited.

"I'm asexual."

I blinked. "What does that mean, exactly? I mean, I've heard the term before, but I don't really get it."

"I don't feel sexual desire. I can have sex, but I don't particularly enjoy it. It's a chore. An obligation. I'd get into a relationship and it would be great, and then she'd want to start having sex. And we would, but I wouldn't be into it, and things would fall apart. Every time, she'd accuse me of cheating or of getting tired of her."

"Why not just be honest?"

"I tried, with one girl. I thought she was the one. But she didn't believe me, told me I needed therapy. Then, when I tried talking to her therapist, he asked if I was sure I'd been doing sex right. He said it was impossible for a man to not want sex. Then he tried to feel me up."

"That's terrible. But I'm sure someone that you were with would have understood."

"That went so badly that I didn't ever want to try again. Plus, the more people I told, the more likely it was for it to go public."

"So?"

"So? I'm an international sex symbol!"

"Why does that matter to you?"

"How could it not? My career depends on it."

"Jeff, you're not an actor anymore. You're a superhero, now."

He blinked at me. "You're right." He laughed. "Oh my gosh, you're right. That never even occurred to me. I was just so used to it being this huge secret."

I stepped toward him and leaned my forehead against his. "You really are a hot mess, aren't you?"

He sighed. "Do you know what the first thing I thought was when I heard about you?"

I shook my head.

"That you'd be woman that I'd never have to make up an excuse not to have sex with." He pulled away from me and buried his face in his hands. "I'd never have to tell you, and things would just work out."

I pulled his hands gently away from his face and wiped away a few tears. Whether or not I could have sex had been one of the harder things for me to get any useful info about—there were too many variables, it was something I really needed a doctor for. And I really didn't want to ask Tabitha to google it for me.

It would be easy to be angry with Jeff. About his secrets, about his assumptions.

His eyes were incredibly blue when he cried. I traced a finger over the barely-there smile lines at the corners of his eyes. "No one goes into a relationship with purely altruistic motivation. You don't need to feel guilty about that."

He stared down at my hands, holding onto his. "You believe me. And you're not mad."

"Seeing that you're not perfect is honestly more of a relief than anything."

"You don't feel betrayed or used?"

"People use each other, Jeff. That's all relationships are — agreements about how we're willing to be used."

"I'm sorry for not trusting you," he said.

"I'm sorry, too."

63

"You can be back on the team," he said.

"I'm pretty sure we decided that I didn't need your permission for that."

"And what about us? Are we still doing this?"

I nodded. "I'm up for it if you are. I just need you to tell me what you want out of a relationship."

"I like kissing and cuddling and—and general intimacy. Romance and feelings and all that. Just not sex."

"Have you really only ever told two people?"

"When I tried to talk about it to my regular therapist, he tried to give me a prescription for Viagra. Then he told me I couldn't be ace because I was physically capable of having sex, and I shouldn't co-opt the identity.

"The worst part was, I wanted him to be right. For a long time, I thought maybe it was something I could get over. That if I just found the right person, I'd finally feel differently. That I'd finally work like a normal person. That I could stop being broken."

I couldn't help wincing at that, and he covered his mouth with both hands. "I'm sorry."

"It's okay. I am broken," I said. "And it's so hard, sometimes. Touch is important. Not being able to feel anything—it's terrible." I reached out and traced his cheek with my fingers. "You're not broken, Jeff."

Tears welled up in his eyes, and I kissed them away. "The only thing that gets me through is focusing on what I do still have instead of on what I've lost. And you're part of what I have now. I—I love you, Jeff."

He kissed me, and I could still taste his tears. "I love you too, Andromeda. Let's move in together."

That sounded fast. But my relationship with Conner had moved so slowly, and that hadn't worked out either. And I did love him. "Okay."

• ○ •

I'd never actually gone to Viv's office before—she'd always come to me. She was sitting behind her desk, looking incredibly professional and leafing through a folder. "How's it going?" I asked. "Any progress on my phone?"

She shook her head. "Apparently they sent one, but it must have gotten lost. I'm requesting a replacement, but it takes time for the paperwork to go through."

I wandered in, looking at the fancy leather-bound books on her shelves. "I think I'm ready to talk to a disability support group."

"Oh, are you having trouble?" Viv asked.

"I think it's time for me to start dealing with things instead of avoiding them."

"I'll get you some info. And hopefully that phone, sometime this century."

"Thanks, Viv. And there's one more thing."

Viv spread her hands, waiting.

"Jeff and I are going to move in together."

Viv's face went blank. "I thought you broke up."

"We talked it out. I know you think it's a bad idea, but I love him, Viv."

She looked angry, and I felt a wave of guilt. "We got through our first fight without anyone cracking," I said. "I think that's a pretty good sign."

I couldn't read the expression on her face. "Well, I'm happy for you, Andromeda. I'll put the paperwork together for you."

I turned to go, feeling oddly unsettled. "Would you mind if I scanned you?" she asked, her voice as oddly blank as her face had been.

I knew she had the right to ask. I couldn't really say no. Plus, I didn't have anything to hide from her.

I gave her my hand.

Pain burned through my entire body, then everything went black.

•○•

I woke in that same tiny room lit with a single lightbulb, strapped to the same chair. Only this time, instead of numb, I felt like I was on fire, like a thousand angry ants were gnawing at every inch of my body.

But I still couldn't feel the chair beneath me. There was nothing but the pain.

Viv sat across the table, glaring.

"What's going on?" I managed. I wanted to believe that this was some crazy misunderstanding, that Viv wasn't behind whatever was wrong with me.

"I thought that was pretty obvious," Viv said. "I knocked you out and strapped you to a chair."

"Why?" I asked. "I thought we were friends." I tried to reach for the restraints with my power, but I couldn't focus through the pain.

"Of course you did. That was part of the plan."

"What plan?" I asked.

She was quiet for a long moment, glaring some more. "You know, I was here first. It's not fair that he'd ignore me and go for you." She leaned forward, so close that I could smell the toothpaste on her breath. "You're not even that pretty."

"Viv, what did you do to me?" I asked. Talking was getting harder, but I felt like this was a very important question.

"I made your nerves talk to your brain again. But just some of them. The pain receptors."

"How?"

"I've been studying your mind."

"How?"

"Did you really think I was paying any attention to that horrible show?"

I wasn't sure if she meant my show or hers. Or both. A spasm shot through me, and I whimpered.

"Yes, I know, I know. I promised." She shrugged. "I lied. I lie a lot. I'm good at it. I was hoping that with enough access, I'd be able to do more than read your thoughts—that I'd be able to shape them." Her hands curled into fists. "But no. Of course not. My power continues to be a disappointment."

I cried out in pain again, and a tiny smile flitted across her face. "Not a complete disappointment, I suppose."

"You're cracked," I gasped, my voice weak and breathy at the edges. I tried my power again, but I couldn't even move my fingers.

"Do you know how long I'd been working to get close to him? But he doesn't like me! Doesn't trust me! And then you show up, and the two of you are thick as thieves instantly. Who wouldn't go crazy faced with that sort of bullshit.

"Do you think it was easy, figuring out a way to kill off the rest of the team? No. It was not. Do you think coming up with a serum to make people lose control of their powers was simple? No! It was so much work, Andromeda! So much. And then you were here, and he was clearly smitten. But I knew how to deal with that. I'd make him have to kill you—after all, that worked last time. But no, you just had to spoil my plan. So instead of us being under house arrest just the two of us, you were still here!

"And I tried to be a good friend to you, I really did. I found you a perfect job! But you turned it down! Then I tried to watch your stupid show and talk you out of dating him, but you just couldn't do the smart thing. You're sort of stupid, I think.

"I didn't want it to come to this. But you just kept rubbing my face in your relationship, and I just can't let that stand."

"What are you going to do to me?"

"I don't know, Andromeda! You've ruined all of my plans! I should just kill you, but I want you to suffer first. Like I've been suffering. I want you to feel the pain I've felt, watching you with him. You and those stupid kids, like you're a family or something. It makes me sick." She stood up. "I'm going to go tell everyone that you ran off. I want you to stay here and think about what you've done."

I didn't even have the strength to scream as she walked out and slammed the door behind her.

● ○ ●

I tried getting angry, but all I could feel was pain. Viv had never been my friend. She'd lied to me and manipulated me, and I'd just blindly trusted her like an idiot. Tears slipped down my cheeks.

At least Jeff and the kids would never believe that I'd run off without saying anything. There was no way that Viv could spin it that they'd buy it.

They'd be looking for me.

But Viv was dangerous. She had that poison, she could inject any one of them with it.

I was trapped in this chair, trapped in my useless body. All I could do was sit and cry.

I imagined Viv injecting Teresa. Imagined the pain and betrayal on her face as her power spiraled out of her control. All she wanted to do was help people.

I imagined Landen burning, his squirrel a cinder on his shoulder. Jackson trying to flee, but falling into the wild flames swirling around him. Jeff fighting his way toward her, wreathed in flames that couldn't hurt him, but facing a task that might break him.

I imagined Tabitha having to turn on her sister to protect the others. Fire against water and leaving only broken ashes.

And that, finally, made me angry. I managed to move one of the straps on the restraints, just a little. I focused on that tiny spark of rage.

"My sister married my fiancé. This pain is nothing." I knew I was lying to myself, but it helped. The strap budged a bit more.

Then Viv came back in. She tugged the leather strap back into place with a snap. "Maybe I should call you Andi, now. Because Andromeda is a superhero, and you're nothing." She ran her fingers through my hair. "This haircut is absurd, you know. And you're entirely too old for it."

"Go to hell."

"I've worked out what I'm going to do with you. I'm going to take you somewhere filled with innocents, inject you with my serum, and let you go. In another city. As much as I want Jeff to be the one to kill you, he might not. He might try to knock you out, instead. And I can't have that. You have to die. Anyway, think about that for a bit. Consider the damage you'll do. How many people you'll hurt. How many you'll kill. I'll be back."

As soon as the door closed, invisible hands tugged on my restraints. "She's completely lost her mind," Jackson said.

I'd never been so relieved to hear the sound of anyone's voice in my entire life.

Once I was no longer strapped to the chair, I slid out of it. "She did something to me," I said. "To my nerves. It hurts, Jackson."

He pulled my arm over his shoulder and lifted. I still couldn't feel his touch. There was only pain. "I've got you, now. Everything is going to be okay."

●○●

The trip out of the basement was a haze of pain and confusion. Jackson half carried, half dragged me up the stairs, and I did my best keep from crying out in pain at every step.

"Where are the others?" I asked. "They need to stay away from Viv."

"What was she talking about, back there? How was she going to make you hurt people?"

"She's the one who's been making people lose control of their powers."

"Shit."

"How much farther is it?" I asked. I didn't want to complain about my rescue, but I really wished we could have taken the elevator.

"It's a ways." Jackson gently set me down. A second later, I could see him. He took my hands. "I think I'm going to have to leave you here. I can go warn the others and send Jeff down for you. I'm not sure if I can carry you all the way up."

"Yes, go," I managed. It was a sensible plan.

Of course, if Viv came back and found me missing, finding me here wouldn't be hard.

But warning the others was more important.

Jackson vanished again, and then he was just a set of footsteps, echoing in the narrow stairway. Then he wasn't even that.

I focused on my breath and tried to ignore the growing fear that no one would be able to fix what Viv had done to me.

I heard a door open, then footsteps approaching. I couldn't move my head to see who was coming.

Viv came into my field of vision slowly, one deliberate step at a time. She was carrying a black pistol, held calmly in both hands. She knelt next to me, shaking her head. "Did you manage to get this far and collapse, or did someone come get you, then abandon you?"

I glared at her.

"I suppose it doesn't matter." She shook her head ruefully. "It's really going to be annoying to get you back into a cell. I should probably just shoot you. I wonder how many bones you'd break if I just pushed you down the stairs."

A door above us slammed open, and someone sprinted toward us. Jeff slid to a halt a few steps above us. "Andromeda," he said. Just that. Just my name. And in spite of the pain and the fear and everything else, I managed to smile at him.

"Oh, don't be disgusting," Viv said. She took a few steps back and pointed the gun at me. "Take one more step and I put a bullet in her brain."

I'd never stopped a bullet.

"What's your end game here, Dr. Sherman?" Jeff asked. "You kill Andromeda, then what?"

I could hear Viv grinding her teeth, but her aim was steady. "I could fix you, you know," she said. "I can do things with nerves. Enhance pain. Or pleasure. I was going to do it slowly. We were going to start spending more time together, and little by little I'd make your body light up whenever we touched."

"I don't need you to fix me. I'm not broken," Jeff said, his voice rough.

"You don't really think that," Viv said.

The gun still didn't waver.

Why hadn't I ever tried stopping a bullet? Jeff had found a tank for me to move, for fuck's sake.

Viv was still talking. "I've read your file. I've studied you. You want what everyone else has. You've always wanted it. You just didn't think you could have it. And so you decided to give up and make a life with the quadriplegic. Look at her. Sitting there, a broken shell. Without her power, she's nothing. You can't honestly tell me that you'd rather shackle yourself to that than come and be with me."

"I love her."

Even if I could stop a bullet normally, I almost certainly wouldn't be able to now.

"You've known her for six months!"

How do guns even work? Was there something inside of it that I could do something to? Guns jammed sometimes, right? How did that happen?

"You're the one I don't know, Dr. Sherman."

Viv heaved one last put-upon sigh. "I really wish that you'd just followed along with my plan. But if everything is going to be ruined, I might as well embrace it."

I embraced all of my pain and my fear and I used it. I was my fear. I was my pain. I reached out toward the gun with my mind, feeling for something, anything, that I could move or break.

Viv pulled the trigger.

I couldn't jam the gun, couldn't stop the bullet. I couldn't even nudge it. My body slammed against the wall as the bullet hit my arm. Right where she'd been aiming. Why was she aiming for my arm?

And then Jeff was on her, pulling the gun out of her hands and crumpling it like a tin can. But her hands were on him, on his wrist, on his cheek, and she was laughing.

Something was wrong. I couldn't feel the bullet wound, but I could feel something. My thin hold over my power broke again, and I felt it coil inside me, like something foreign. Like a snake, preparing to strike.

"Jeff, you have to run," I said. My voice sounded thick and far away. Everything hurt, and I couldn't hold on. "She put her poison on the bullet."

I willed myself to pass out. The pain was constant and oppressive. I'd been shot.

Unconsciousness wasn't a lot to ask.

The building started to shake.

I knew I was doing it, but I couldn't stop it.

I thought about Terrence O'Reily. "Jeff, please," I said. "You have to go."

Viv floated up into the air. I fought against my power, tried to put her back down, but I couldn't control it. I couldn't control anything.

Viv was still laughing. My power pulled her body apart at the joints, and her blood sprayed out into the air, where it hung like huge soap bubbles.

I screamed.

More footsteps sounded above us.

The kids were coming.

I wondered where Jeff was, but couldn't look for him. Then I tried not to think of him, in case that pointed my power in his direction.

I blinked away tears, and my power caught them so that they floated toward the lazily drifting blood.

I'd killed Viv, but she'd at least deserved it. If I hurt Jeff or one of the kids—my mind recoiled from the thought.

Then, hundreds of tiny bodies burst into my awareness, and the sound of flapping wings filled the air. My power caught some of them, but there were too many. A bird landed on my shoulder and pecked at the bullet wound. Then there was another, and another. Wings buffeted me, and feathers floated with the blood. Some of it was mine, now.

Then finally, finally, everything went black.

•○•

I floated in and out of awareness, unable to move. I had nightmares about pulling Viv apart, about pulling everyone I cared about apart. Cassie's face ripped like a cheap Halloween mask, Tabitha crumpled like tissue paper. Jeff shredded into a thousand uneven chunks of flesh and bone.

I had nightmares where birds pecked out my eyes and I could still see pools of blood floating through the air.

When I finally woke up, I was in a hospital bed. I couldn't feel anything, and I sobbed in pure relief.

Jeff was sitting next to the bed, staring down into a Styrofoam cup.

"Hey," I said.

"Hey." He sat the cup down and took one of my hands. "How are you feeling?"

"Better," I said. "How did you get the pain to stop?"

"We called in one of the elite teams for help. They have a telepath on their team, and he poked around in your brain and managed to fix what Dr. Sherman did in there." He took a deep breath. "You should be okay, now."

I'd never felt so relived in my life.

"There's a chance that he might be able to do more than that. He thinks that he might be able use what he learned from looking at what Dr. Sherman did to partially restore your sense of touch. It won't be the same as it was, but it might be something."

"That would be amazing," I said.

Jeff smiled. "I figured you'd say that, but your sister is still listed as your emergency contact, and she wanted them to wake you up to ask. There are risks. You'll be able to feel pain again, if you get hurt. And pressure. But probably not heat or cold or subtle things like texture."

"Something is better than nothing. Are you okay with it?" I asked.

"It's your body Andromeda. I support you no matter what."

"And we'll still be okay, if it works?"

He nodded. "I already moved all of our stuff into one of the double rooms. I'm not breaking up with you after all that work."

"Yeah, I know how difficult carrying things is for you."

He ran his thumb along my cheek. "They'll have to put you back under soon."

"Okay. Tell the kids that they did a great job, and that I'll see them soon. Thank them for me."

He kissed me. "I love you."

"I love you, too."

• ○ •

I woke up in a hospital room, feeling indescribably weird, surrounded by familiar faces. Jeff, Tabitha, Teresa, Landen and Jackson all stood together on my right. Conner and Cassie stood on my left. I'd thought of them as my future and my past. But here they all were, in the present.

They were all staring, and I managed a faint smile. "Tell me it's been less than two years, this time."

"It's felt like it," Jeff said. "But it's only been a week." He looked like he hadn't slept in that entire time.

My sense of touch felt distant and faint, like an echo of a whisper. I could feel my weight, pressing into the bed, but not the hospital gown or sheets against my skin. But it was something. And my power was back, so I used it to lift my hand. I threaded my fingers through Jeff's and squeezed.

And when he squeezed back, I could feel it.

73

This story is set in the same world as *Andromeda Snow: Superhero*. I wrote it as part of *Second Revolution*, my recent flash fiction collection and wanted to include it here as a bonus story. Enjoy!

THE NEW NORMAL

Joseph ran up his front steps two at a time. "Meena? I'm home, where are you?" She wasn't in the kitchen, or her office, or the bedroom. "Honey? I got your text, what's going on?"

He found her phone, plugged in next to the bed, still showing her message—*I need you, come home now*—and all of his unread, increasingly frantic replies.

He found her in the garden, surrounded by what looked like all of the deer that roamed their suburban neighborhood and a few stray cats.

"They're mine now. I can see through all of their eyes, make them do what I want," she said as he rushed out of the house. "I want to see if you can be mine, too."

She took his hand, and everything around him wobbled.

Her laugh sounded like it came from everywhere. "I can! This is amazing! What else can I do?"

A tiny, unimportant corner of his mind realized that she had superpowers, now, and that the sudden strain had cracked her, like it had so many others since the Emergence.

He stood by while she pulled more and more creatures under her thrall, till she attracted the notice of the local team of super heroes.

Then she used him, just like everything else that she controlled, when the heroes fought her.

Then she was in a crumpled heap on the ground, and everything went black.

• ○ •

Joseph went through all the right motions at the funeral. He shook hands, hugged people, nodded when they offered condolences.

He might even have shed a tear or two at the appropriate moments, he wasn't sure. When it was all over, he couldn't really remember much of it.

The doctors said that his mind would return to normal, eventually. That his life would stop feeling like something he was watching without much interest instead of something that he was living.

That eventually, he wouldn't be Meena's anymore.

"Do you want me to take you home?" Stewart, his best friend, asked when everyone else had gone.

Joseph shrugged. He knew he should care, or at least pretend to, but he was tired. He's been pretending to care all day.

"Meena really did a number on you, huh," Stewart said, taking Joseph's arm and clearly not expecting an answer as he guided him to the car. "Super scary, what supers can do when they crack."

Joseph grunted in agreement. It was scary, he supposed. It hadn't felt scary at the time though. He'd been a part of something larger than himself, and he'd felt... complete.

Stewart took him home and made him some scrambled eggs. "Look, man, I know things are hard for you right now, but I'm here. You know that, right? I can stay with you for as long as you need me."

Joseph nodded. He did know.

"Do you want to talk or anything?"

"Not yet." Maybe not ever. He wasn't sure.

"How about we watch a movie, then? Something to get you out of your own head for a bit."

"Yeah. That sounds good."

• ○ •

The deer and cats and other creatures that Meena had pulled in were still hanging around the yard. If Joseph hadn't fully thrown off her hold yet, how could the animals hope to do it?

He liked having them there. It made him feel a little more whole.

Then one morning, Stewart found him sleeping on the ground outside, curled between two deer with a vole or something tucked under his chin. Joseph didn't remember going outside. But he already knew that his memory wasn't the best.

"This is worrying." Stewart said, making more eggs. "I mean, even aside from the weird brain stuff. What about fleas? Or ticks? You do not want Lyme disease on top of everything else."

One of the pack was a possum, he remembered. Possums ate ticks, right? He should be able to have it check on the others.

Joseph opened his mouth to tell Stewart that, then stopped. "I think you should take me to get tested," he said instead.

"Tested for Lyme?"

"No, for super powers."

• ○ •

Stewart quietly let the nurse make some very wrong assumptions about their relationship so that he could stay in the room while Joseph waited for the doctor. "I'd understand if you didn't want to stay," he said.

"Not everyone cracks," Stewart said. "I trust you."

"I trusted Meena."

Stewart shrugged. "What she did was messed up, but I don't think she meant to hurt you."

"Yeah, so even if I didn't mean to hurt you, things could still get pretty bad."

"I'm not going anywhere. I said I was here for you, and I meant it." They sat in silence for a moment. Then Stewart added, "This is probably better than talking about feelings, anyway."

Joseph laughed. "You're so full of shit."

The test was straightforward, but the results were inconclusive. "Well, something weird is going on," the doctor said. "It's unclear if you're manifesting a separate power of your own, or if this development is a lingering result of your wife's influence."

"I'm not getting any better."

"We can schedule regular appointments to monitor the situation, but at the moment, I don't feel like any further action is necessary."

• ○ •

Joseph sat out on the porch, surrounded by his animals. He wondered when he'd stopped thinking of them as Meena's.

77

Stewart brought him a beer. "You're wrong about one thing, you know," he said.

"What's that?"

"You are getting better. Like, the weird animal thing isn't going away, but you're—you're better than you were. Not so far away anymore. You actually laughed today. I can't remember the last time that happened. Maybe the menagerie is doing you some good."

"Having a psychic connection with a bunch of deer has to be the stupidest superpower ever."

"Now, now. It's not just deer. There are also some rodents and a few cats."

"You're right. That definitely makes it better."

They sat on the porch, surrounded by Joseph's menagerie of suburban wildlife, and watched the sun go down. "Here's to the new normal," Stewart toasted.

Joseph nodded once, and clinked his bottle against Stewart's. Things weren't good, yet. But they certainly could be worse. "To the new normal."

○ ● ○

Kickstarter Backers

Jenn Scott
Savannah Bozonier
Paul Stefko
Patrick J. Ropp
Mary Soon Lee
Todd Sanders
Elizabeth Jones
Laine Wilson
Chris Aumiller
Jeremy Zimmerman
Julie J. Tennis
Lois Stefko
Betsy Bodamer
Chuck Santistevan
Karen Herkes
Linda McNair
Amy Treadwell
Barbara Carlson
Frank Oreto
Brooke Ardile
Beth Morris Tanner
Larry Ivkovich
Alexis P.
Vicky Boardley
Darren Radford
Douglas Gwilym
Aaron M. Roth
Celeste Tronka
MikeBrendan
Tracey Levino

Megan Lynch
John Thompson
Ross Pollock
Christopher Niessl
George Stankow
Andy Rehder
Aimee Picchi
Hammond Diehl
Matthew Lackey
Jaq Greenspon
Carl Rigney
Cory Livingston
Bill Waugh
Damon Griffin
If This Goes On (Don't Panic)
Pete Butler-Davis
Julia Mulligan
Alex Shvartsman
Rebecca Young
Sergey Kochergan
Carissa Lackey
Diane Turnshek
Joseph Benedetto
Sherry Mock
Elizabeth Prager
Clairice C
Ken Chiacchia
Michael A. Burstein
Don and Debbie Lackey